THE OFFICIAL PRO FOOTBALL HALL OF FAME PLAY BOOK

Rick Korch

SIMON AND SCHUSTER BOOKS FOR YOUNG READERS
Published by Simon & Schuster Inc.
New York

The views expressed in this book are solely
those of the author and do not necessarily
represent those of the Pro Football Hall of Fame.

Photos appear courtesy of NFL Properties, Inc.,
and the Pro Football Hall of Fame.

A TOUCHDOWN PUBLICATIONS BOOK

SIMON AND SCHUSTER
BOOKS FOR YOUNG READERS
Simon & Schuster Building
Rockefeller Center
1230 Avenue of the Americas
New York, NY 10020

Also available in a Little Simon paperback edition
Manufactured in the United States of America
10 9 8 7 6 5 4 3 2 1
ISBN: 0-671-71002-8
0-671-68698-4 (pbk)

Contents

Introduction

You've seen it happen lots of times. Your favorite team comes out of the huddle. It lines up in its normal formation. The quarterback yells out a few calls. The center snaps the ball. The quarterback hands the ball off to the halfback, and he runs around the right end behind the blocks of two guards and the fullback. He goes about four yards before being tackled by the opposing team's middle linebacker and safety.

Simple, isn't it?

Not really.

Each of the eleven players on offense has a role defined by the instructions that the quarterback gives in the huddle. Each man must know (1) the formation, (2) the play, (3) whether the tight end is lined up on the left or right side of the line, and (4) the snap count. Then, at the line of scrimmage, the quarterback will "read" the defense and bark out additional signals. If the defense shifts, the center will shout out calls to the other linemen to modify their blocks. And while all this is happening on the offensive side of the line before the ball is snapped, equally complex moves are taking place among the defenders.

All the same, even the most complicated plays in a pro football game have their roots in the games played in the playgrounds and backyards of youth: A quarterback finds a dusty spot in the grass and sketches out assignments—"Jimmy, you line up on the right, take seven steps downfield, then cut to the sideline. Bobby, you go deep. The rest of you, hold your blocks." As these players become older, stronger, and faster, they may enter organized play and learn more detailed plays from their coaches.

By the time the very best players reach the professional ranks, they have played for several coaches and learned hundreds of plays and variations. The ones their NFL coach wants them to learn for a given year are recorded in the team's playbook.

At first glance, the playbooks for most NFL teams look the same, but they differ a lot in terminology. A closer look shows they also differ in philosophy, strategy, and game plan. Teams change as much as 30 or 40 percent of their playbook from season to season.

The typical fan probably wouldn't understand much in a pro football team's playbook. We'll try to explain this "hidden game" as simply as possible, and before you know it, you will know which is the "three hole" and where the "gaps" are,

Miami Dolphin quarterback Dan Marino calls an audible.

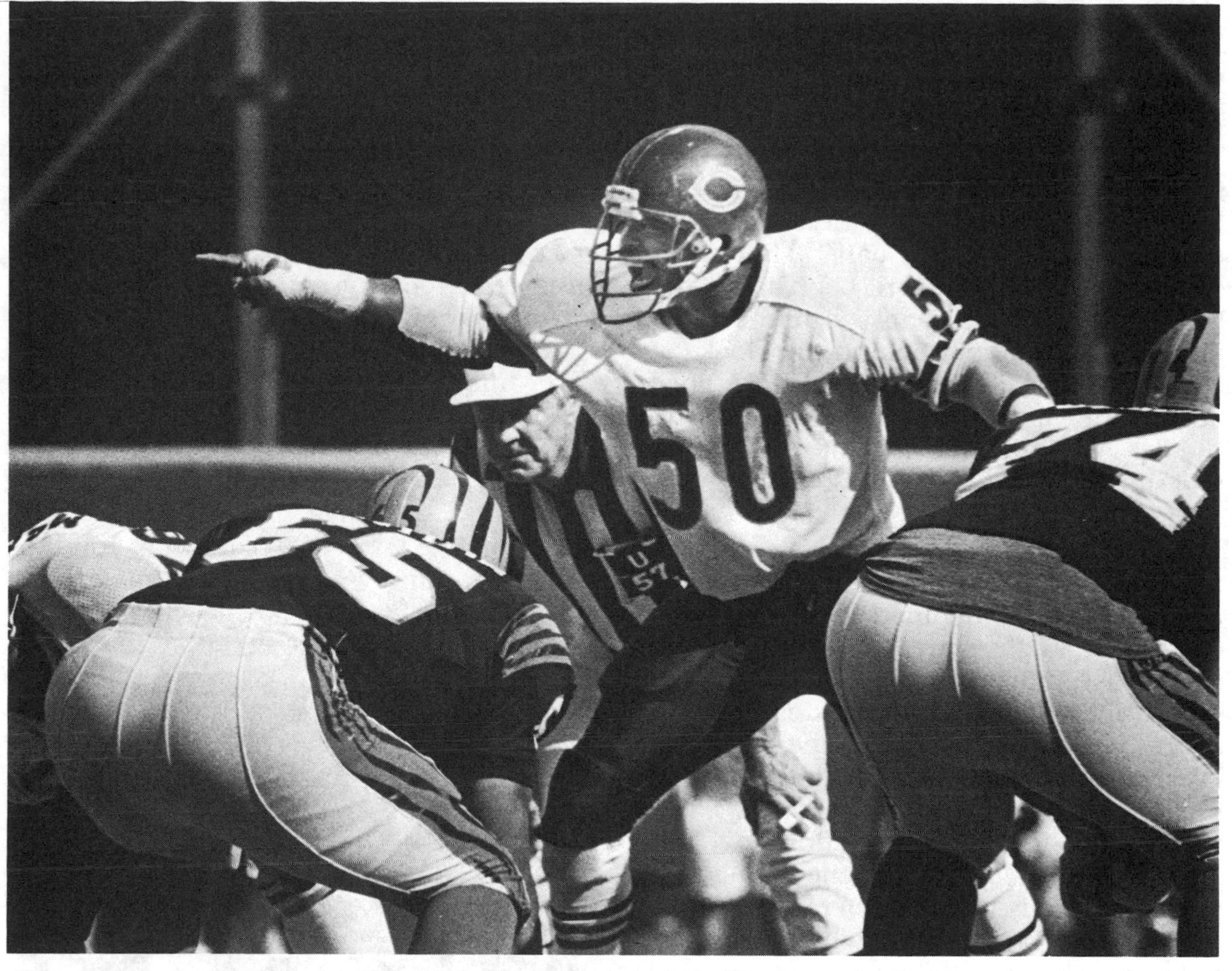

Chicago Bears middle linebacker and defensive captain, Mike Singletary, calls signals.

the difference between "stunts" and "stacks," and maybe even what the "keys" are for "pluggers" to "blitz." At the end of the book is a glossary in which many of the unfamiliar terms of pro football are explained.

You will have a better understanding and a greater knowledge about what your favorite team is doing out there. That's what this book is all about: a compilation of the basic plays that all teams use, along with a selection of favorite plays from some of today's head coaches.

No other team sport depends so much on teamwork. Eleven players have to work together at the same time to achieve the same goal—scoring or keeping the opposing team from scoring. Almost every coach teaches the same plays. As Vince Lombardi once said, football is nothing more than running and jumping, blocking and tackling, throwing and catching. But some coaches have players who can do a better job of understanding and *executing* the strategies and formations, tactics and techniques, shotguns and blitzes, overs and unders, bombs and flares, H-backs and nickel backs, dimes and quarters, zones and gadgets, T-formations, I-formations, and pro sets.

Football requires more than speed and size—it takes brains, too, as you will see in this playbook, this guide to the game inside the game.

CHAPTER ONE

The Game

In the NFL, rookies are expected to learn their playbook before they report for their first training camp. Veterans don't need to look at them as much as rookies because so many plays carry over from the previous season, unless the team has a change in coaches.

At first, all a rookie cares about is learning his own assignments—what he is supposed to do on a certain play. Later on, he begins to learn the entire play—what everybody else is doing, both on offense and defense. For example, a rookie wide receiver will at first learn what route to run on a pass play. Later, he learns what routes the other receivers are running. Then he is able to adjust his moves when the primary receiver (the one who is supposed to get the pass) is covered.

The quarterback is probably the only player who needs to know the entire playbook, but the best players usually know what everyone else is doing.

A playbook is a player's dictionary. In the NFL, a player is fined $500 or even $1,000 if his playbook is lost or stolen.

There are separate playbooks for offense and defense. The offense's playbook lists things like quarterback calls, the huddle, terminology, the play-numbering system, the numbering of the backs, formations (both offensive and defensive, so the offensive players can learn to recognize defenses), the two-minute drill, the automatic or checkoff system at the line, and the means of calling signals. It also lists hundreds of plays and variations of each play. The defense's playbook lists such things as the prevent scoring theory, pass defense theory (which concerns man-to-man or zone preferences), and the theory of blitzing. The defense's playbook is concerned mainly with stopping the offense.

The more conservative coaches in the NFL—those who don't get very fancy—may have only about 60 to 75 running plays in their books and about the same number of passes. Teams that run a multiple offense, such as the Denver Broncos and the San Francisco 49ers, have many more. Altogether, though, the pros use fewer than 500 plays.

What determines which play to call? Basically, coaches try to use their team's strengths against their opponents' weaknesses. To analyze their opponents, coaches use statistics, computers, charts showing opponents' tendencies on certain downs with differing distances needed for a first, scouting reports, and film of the opponents' previous games. Before each game, coaches try to determine which plays will have the greatest success, both offensively and defensively. This information is all worked up into a game plan.

Down-and-distance dictates to the greatest extent what kind of offensive play is going to be called. For example, you can usually expect a plunge over the middle on third-and-one, and almost always a pass on third-and-ten.

Quarterbacks call the plays, but they don't always *select* them. Today, plays are usually called by the offensive coordinator, with assistance from an offensive assistant coach in the press box, connected by telephone to the sideline. Plays are often sent in through a messenger, such as a guard or a tight end going in for the play, or through hand signals from the sidelines. Defensive plays are more often sent in by hand signals from the defensive coordina-

Field Position: Conventional Strategy

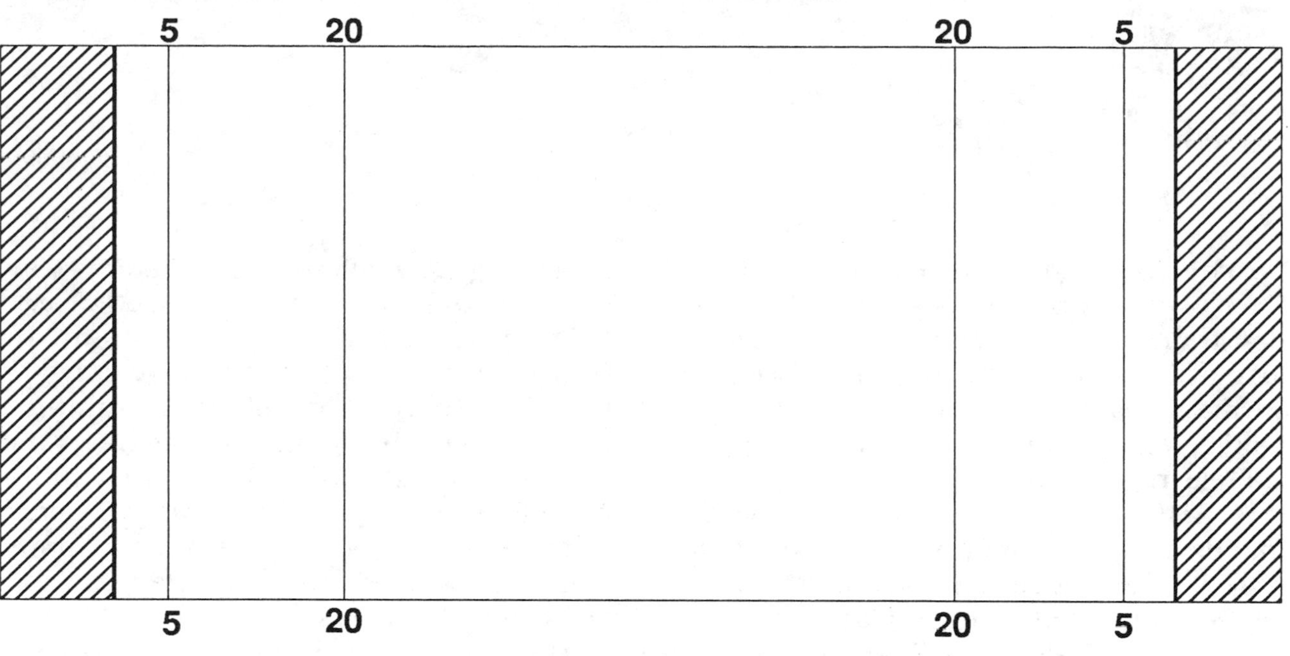

5-yard line to goal line—On offense, use your best running plays straight at the defense, or play-action passes where you fake a run and throw a pass with your receivers crossing. Substitute bigger tight ends for small wide receivers. On defense, substitute bigger players for running plays and defensive backs capable of playing both the run and the pass.

20-yard line to 5-yard line—The offense is in scoring position on every play. Go with basic plays that have a good chance to gain big yards, but also have little chance of losing yardage. Don't lose your fourth-down field-goal range, and, even more important, don't make a turnover. The defense shouldn't gamble too much because it could give up a score, but should attack the ball in the hope of creating a turnover. Giving up only a field goal here is good.

Between the 20s—On offense, this is where you can try anything, and where you want to probe the defense to see what will work. Use a variety of run and pass plays, mixing in different formations. On defense, you don't want to let up the big play because it could lead to a score, but you can gamble with blitzes and other tricks.

5-yard line to 20-yard line—The offense goes with its basic plays that assure against losing yardage. The defense can go all-out, gambling on the possibility that the offense will make a mistake.

Goal line to 5-yard line—On offense, use conservative plays to get out of trouble, such as quick-hitting running plays. Pass blocking has to be for maximum protection so the quarterback doesn't get sacked. On defense, a gamble could pay off in safety or a turnover, but you also don't want to give up a big play that takes the offense out of danger. Blitzes are big here.

tor, although substitutes frequently bring a play in with them.

On running plays, the side with the tight end is the strongside because the tight end gives the offense an extra blocker. (If there are two tight ends, the coach designates one of them as the strongside.) On passing plays, however, the number of receivers determines the strongside. The side with the two receivers is strong, and it may or may not be the tight end's side.

On the other hand, every defensive formation is both strong *and* weak. That's why TV announcers will say, "the defense always gives the offense something to attack." Here's why: To support against the run, a team exposes its defensive backs to the pass. To overprotect one side of the field, it must underman another side.

If there is one secret to play selection—offense or defense—it is the instinct to attack at the points of least resistance. Coaches are just like generals in a war.

Here is each player's responsibility:

OFFENSE

Quarterback. Quarterbacks call the signals and are the primary ballhandlers. They hand off to the running backs, pass to the receivers, and occasionally run with the ball. Quarterbacks usually get all the credit or all the blame. In sports, the quarterback's position is unique. He is involved in every offensive play, both before and during its execution.

Running backs. Most backfields have a halfback and a fullback though both of them may sometimes be designated simply as running backs. The halfback does everything—he runs with the ball, catches passes, blocks, and sometimes throws passes. The fullback is bigger than the halfback, and usually lines up on the same side as the tight end. He has to be a good blocker and pass receiver too.

Running backs are the most instinctive players in football. Most great runners will tell you they don't know how they do what they do—they just do it. Running backs are also an important part of the passing scheme. Backs usually run patterns in the areas underneath the wide receiver routes and *act as "safety valves"*—somebody the quarterback can pass to in case the wide receivers are covered. They should *force the linebackers* to cover them instead of allowing the linebackers to drop back and help their secondary cover the wide receivers or try to rush the quarterback. They are also *pass blockers*, checking to see if any linebackers are rushing before going into their pass patterns.

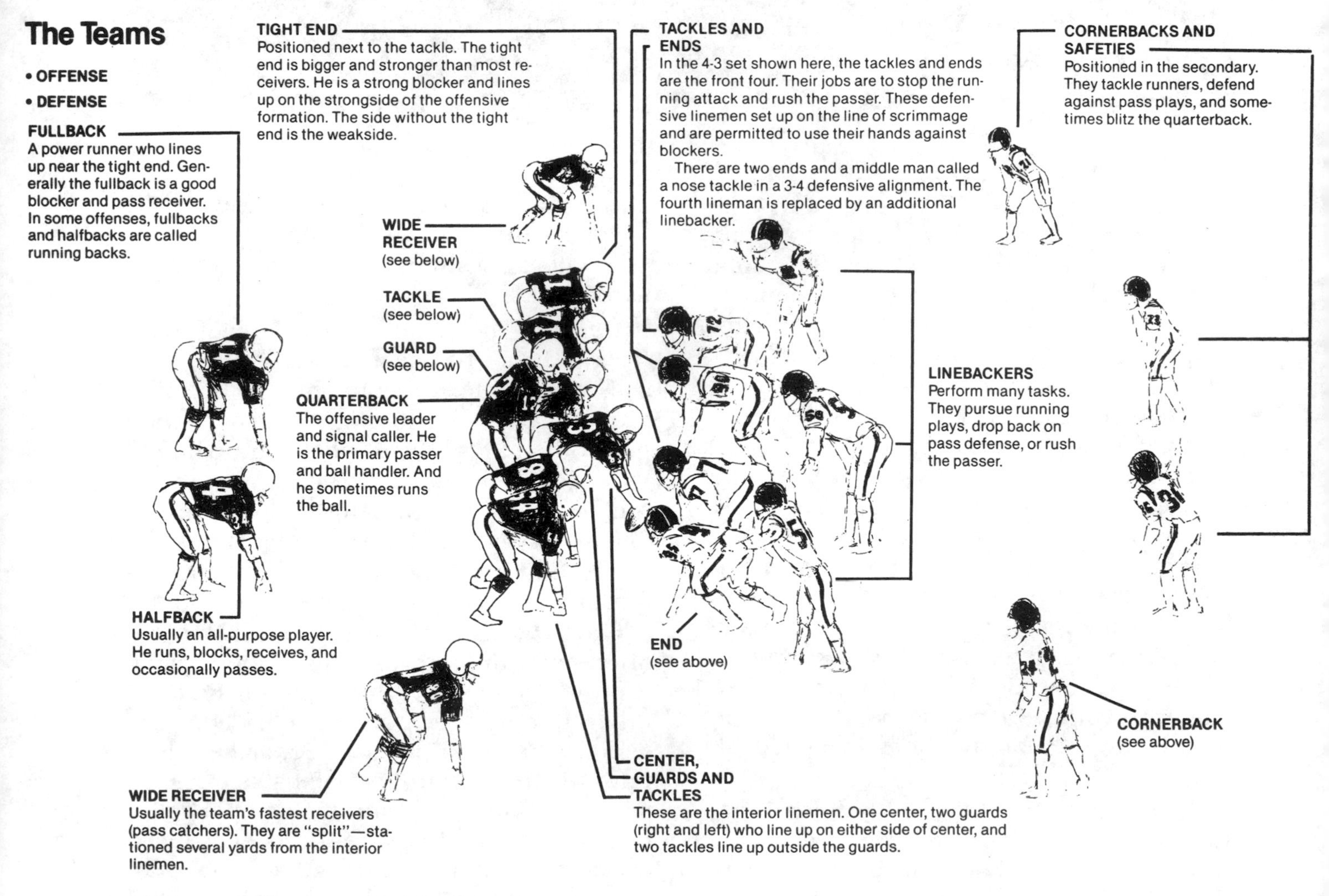
The Teams
• OFFENSE
• DEFENSE
FULLBACK
A power runner who lines up near the tight end. Generally the fullback is a good blocker and pass receiver. In some offenses, fullbacks and halfbacks are called running backs.
TIGHT END
Positioned next to the tackle. The tight end is bigger and stronger than most receivers. He is a strong blocker and lines up on the strongside of the offensive formation. The side without the tight end is the weakside.
WIDE RECEIVER
(see below)
TACKLE
(see below)
GUARD
(see below)
QUARTERBACK
The offensive leader and signal caller. He is the primary passer and ball handler. And he sometimes runs the ball.
HALFBACK
Usually an all-purpose player. He runs, blocks, receives, and occasionally passes.
WIDE RECEIVER
Usually the team's fastest receivers (pass catchers). They are "split"—stationed several yards from the interior linemen.
TACKLES AND ENDS
In the 4-3 set shown here, the tackles and ends are the front four. Their jobs are to stop the running attack and rush the passer. These defensive linemen set up on the line of scrimmage and are permitted to use their hands against blockers.
There are two ends and a middle man called a nose tackle in a 3-4 defensive alignment. The fourth lineman is replaced by an additional linebacker.
CORNERBACKS AND SAFETIES
Positioned in the secondary. They tackle runners, defend against pass plays, and sometimes blitz the quarterback.
LINEBACKERS
Perform many tasks. They pursue running plays, drop back on pass defense, or rush the passer.
END
(see above)
CORNERBACK
(see above)
CENTER, GUARDS AND TACKLES
These are the interior linemen. One center, two guards (right and left) who line up on either side of center, and two tackles line up outside the guards.

Diagram of offensive and defensive players.

Hall of Famer Fran Tarkenton calls signals for the Vikings.

Wide receivers. There are two basic wide receivers, though in some situations there may be as many as four. The split end—the end "split off" from the offensive line—is positioned *on* the line of scrimmage, bringing the number of players there to the required seven. He is usually lined up opposite the tight end and is usually separated from the rest of the line by a few yards. The second wide receiver, the flanker, can line up in many places *behind* the line of scrimmage, usually a step back. If he is between the split end and the tackle, he's said to be in a "slot" formation. He often goes into motion. How wide he lines up is determined by the play. In obvious passing downs, a team may also dispense with its running backs and line up two additional receivers in slot positions.

Tight end. The tight end is a combination offensive tackle and wide receiver. He has to be strong enough to block a defensive player and mobile enough to run a pattern and catch a pass. Today, they'll occasionally line up wide, whereas 15 years ago they almost always lined up next to the tackle.

Center. The center snaps the ball, then tries to block the nose tackle, all by himself, if possible. A center has to be big—and quick enough to make the snap, then get both hands up to block immediately with a 270-pound defensive lineman intent on crashing into him. Some teams keep a specialist for the long snaps for punts and extra-point and field-goal attempts.

Guards. Guards are the most agile offensive linemen because they move around to block more frequently than other linemen. A guard might help the center ward off a nose tackle, or he might have to face a charging defensive end or a surprise assault from an inside linebacker or a safety. The basic qualities of a guard are: The power to fire out at the man across from him on a straight-ahead run-

ning play; the quickness to move sideways rather than straight ahead on a running play requiring deception and delay; the speed to get out of his stance in a hurry and pull outside on a flip pass to a running back on a wide running play; and the grit to hold his position and fight a pass rusher to a standoff on a dropback pass by the quarterback.

Tackles. Tackles are the pillar of a strong running team. They are the biggest, toughest, and slowest players on offense. Tackles are mostly straight-ahead blockers, but occasionally they pull across toward the opposite end. On a pass play the tackle protects the space inside, which is the key to the quarterback's protective "pocket"—the place where he can, for a second or two, have an unobstructed view of his receivers. The left tackle has the hardest job on the offensive line. He faces the best pass rusher and is blocking the quarterback's "blind side" (if the quarterback is right-handed).

DEFENSE

Defensive ends. On plays toward the middle, defensive ends keep the ballcarrier inside. On sweeps (wide running plays), they try to force the ballcarrier even wider, ideally out-of-bounds. They are the best pass rushers on the defensive line.

Defensive tackles. Two defensive tackles play in a 4–3 defense. They try to force the pocket deep on pass plays and deny openings up the middle on runs, preventing the runner from bursting through a "hole" in the line.

Nose tackle. In a defense with 3 men on the line, there is a lone tackle usually lined up head-on with the center, or "nose-to-nose"—thus, "nose tackle." He is almost always double-teamed by the center and a guard, so the nose tackle's job is to tie up the two offensive linemen so other defensive players can make the tackles.

Dallas Cowboy running back Drew Hill runs the sweep.

Pittsburgh Steeler Hall of Famer "Mean" Joe Greene rushes the passer.

Linebackers. Linebackers are the essential part of the defense against the run and an integral part against the pass. There is one basic difference between defensive linemen and linebackers: On the snap of the ball, the lineman acts and *then* "reads" or diagnoses; the linebacker reads and then acts. The strongside linebacker often lines up as an extra lineman, usually across from the tight end. His job is to stop the run, jamming up the center and the guards. He is also the first player to be replaced in an obvious passing situation, when his team goes to a "nickel" defense (five defensive backs). The weakside linebacker is usually the best pass rusher of the linebacking unit and the most dominant player on the defense. He is often assigned to cover a running back. The inside linebackers guard against both the run and the pass.

Today's most flamboyant and feared defensive players are linebackers, especially those on the outside. In the old days, the middle linebacker was the glamour position; now it's the outside linebacker, especially the weak outside linebacker, like Lawrence Taylor of the New York Giants.

Cornerbacks. A game is usually won or lost depending on how well a cornerback stops his man, says Hall of Fame cornerback Willie Brown of the Los Angeles Raiders. The two cornerbacks, who line up behind the linebackers, have to be able to tackle bigger runners. They must also have the speed to cover the fast receivers to whom they are assigned on pass plays, or the areas they are assigned to patrol when the pass coverage is not "man-to-man" but "zone."

Safeties. The two safeties are called "strong" and "free" (or "weak"). The free safety is free to pursue the ball since he doesn't usually have man-to-man coverage responsibilities. The strong safety usually plays against the tight end. He plays as a defensive back against the pass and as another linebacker against the run. The safeties are the "last line of defense" in a deep pass play—if a receiver gets behind a cornerback, and the safety fails to provide help, the result is usually a touchdown.

CHAPTER TWO

The Evolution of the Offense

The pro set is the offensive formation you usually see on television, and it has been the basic formation in the NFL for almost 30 years. It's easy to distinguish because it has two running backs, two wide receivers, and a tight end. But it took nearly 50 years to develop.

Let's review a bit of football history to see how we arrived at the game of today. You will see how offensive formations changed in response to defensive innovations and how, especially, the passing game developed as defenses learned to close down the run.

SINGLE WING

The single wing was used for almost 50 years after it was invented—around 1906—by Pop Warner. He was the famed coach of Carlisle and Stanford for whom today's largest youth football leagues are named. The single wing enabled the offense to trick the defense with a lot of spins and reverses, but its main value was in concentrating great power at the point of attack on running plays. In the diagram on page 10, see how the tailback (B), after

Legend

●	Offensive player (other than center)	▼	Defensive lineman
C	Center	■	Linebacker or defensive back
G	Offensive guard	E	Defensive end
T	Offensive tackle	T	Defensive tackle
X	Wide receiver	N	Nose tackle
Y	Tight end	L	Linebacker
Z	Wide receiver (flanker)	C	Cornerback
Q	Quarterback	S	Safety
H	Halfback	N	Nickel back (fifth defensive back)
F	Fullback	D	Dime back (sixth defensive back)
	Block		

receiving the ball from center, has three blockers escorting him around right end—a pulling tackle (T), the fullback (F), and the quarterback (Q). These three blockers bear down on a lone defensive back, while the wingback (W) seals off the defensive end.

The single wing was not football's first formation. That was the primitive T formation invented by Walter Camp in the 1880s. But the T was designed for power, not deception, and it gave way to the single wing by 1910 (only to be revived in a new format in the 1930s). The single wing is very similar to the Green Bay Packers' power sweep of the 1960s. Pass plays were nearly nonexistent in the early days of pro football, so the single wing dominated. Note that the person taking the ball from the center was several yards back, rather than being right behind the center. In those days, he was called the tailback.

Single Wing

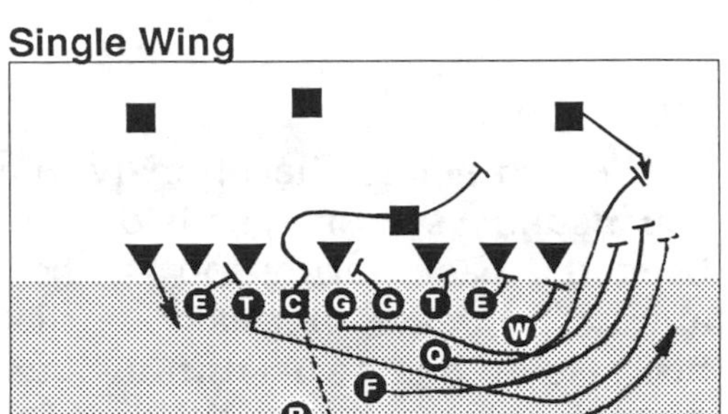

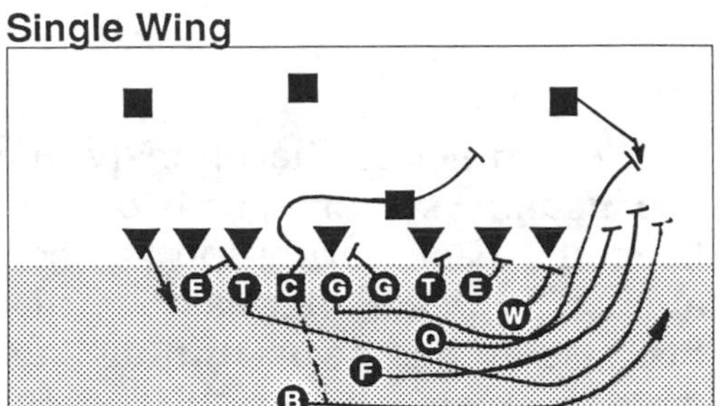

DOUBLE WING

The double wing play was used a lot by Pop Warner at Carlisle when he had one of the all-time legends, Jim Thorpe, in his backfield, and at Stanford in the late 1920s. The double wing laid the foundation for pass plays from spread formations—such as the shotgun, which became popular almost 50 years later—because it removed two men from the backfield to put two receivers on each side.

Double Wing

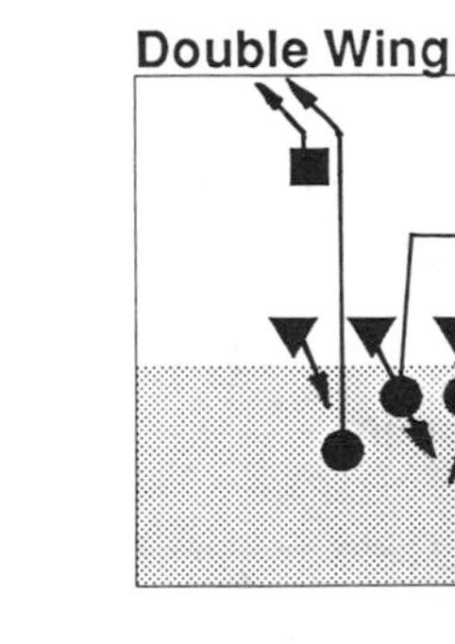

TRIPLE WING

The triple wing is similar to the double wing, but it places three receivers to one side of the center. The double wing and the triple wing are still used today in different variations.

Triple Wing

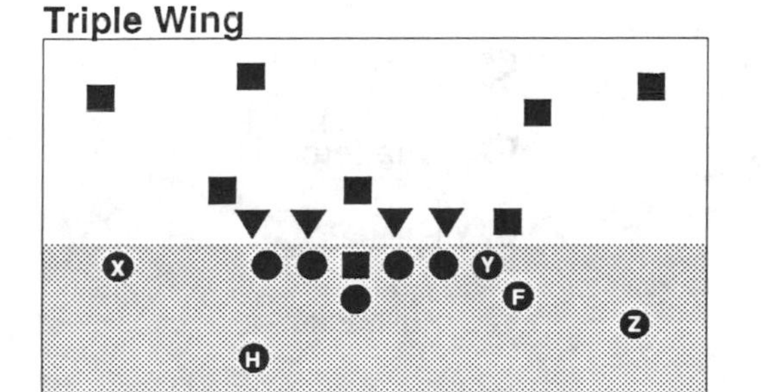

A-FORMATION

Steve Owen, coach of the New York Giants from 1937 to 1952, developed the A-formation, which had unusual line splits, a line strong to one side and the backfield strong to the other, and a direct snap to the left halfback rather than to a quarterback. It split the running backs out farther than they had been before.

A-formation

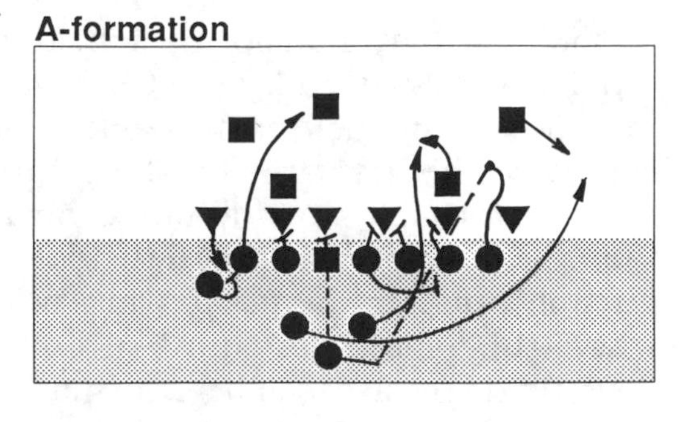

NOTRE DAME BOX

Legendary Notre Dame coach Knute Rockne devised the Notre Dame box about 1920. The Fighting Irish would shift from a primitive T-formation to their box and then take off on an end run, practically all in one motion, while the ball was being hiked to a halfback. Rules were eventually changed so that offensive players had to be still for a full second before the snap.

Notre Dame Box

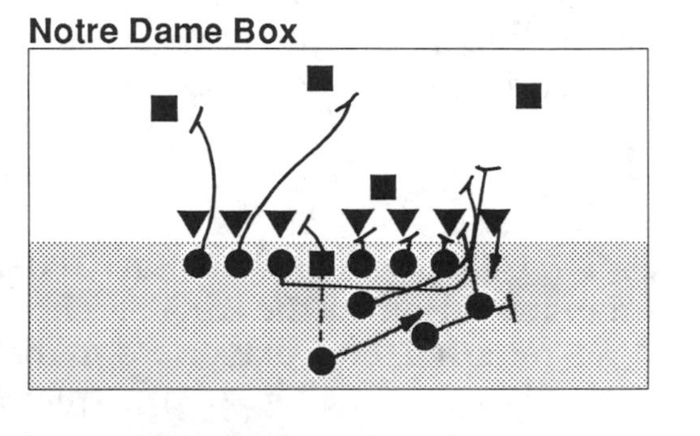

MAN IN MOTION

All but one offensive player must be stationary at the time the ball is snapped. The player who runs across the field behind the line of scrimmage is the man in motion. He can be a wide receiver, tight end, or running back. Putting a man in motion has been around since the turn of the century. It allows the offense to do more things, such as putting a running back closer to the outside before the play begins. There he can take a quick pitchout or serve as a lead blocker. It also forces the defense to make adjustments.

Man in Motion

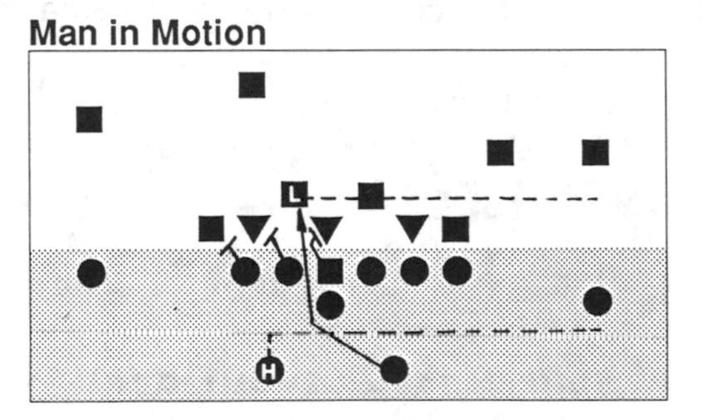

T-FORMATION

Now the dominant formation, the modern T was first used by the Chicago Bears in 1930. It put the quarterback under the center for the first time (in the primitive T the quarterback stood about a yard away from the center) and spread the defense by putting smaller, faster players out wide where they could get running room or go downfield for passes. The T-formation was really popularized after the Chicago Bears used it to defeat the Washington Redskins 73–0 in the 1940 NFL championship game. Within 10 years, nearly every team at the college and pro level had changed to the T. It has been the basis for most offensive strategies in the last 50 years.

T-formation

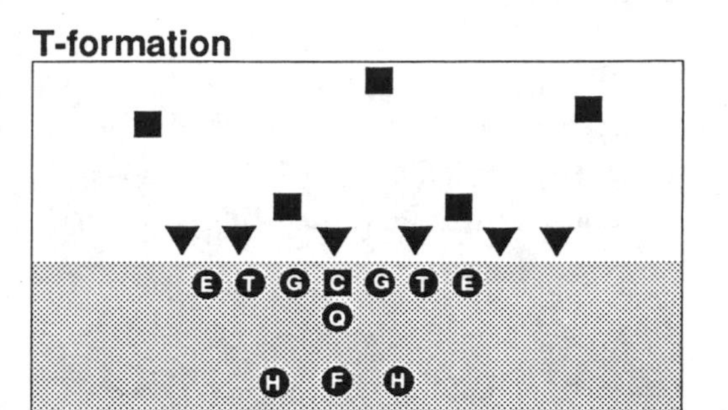

SLOT-T

The Chicago Bears had started using the man-in-motion in the 1930s. This formation removed one player from the backfield. By the late '40s, that player was being permanently stationed out wide. He became the flanker, and was usually stationed between the tackle and the split end. Eventually, the flanker came to be seen not as a halfback removed from the backfield, but rather as a third receiver. Later, the terms wide receiver and tight end were adopted to designate the other two receivers.

Slot-T

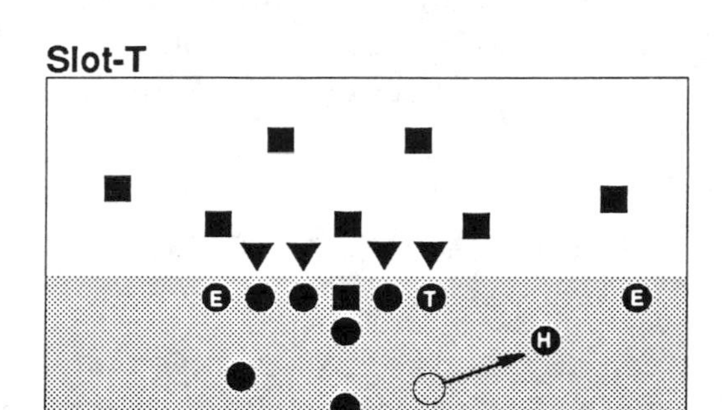

OTHER VARIATIONS OF THE T-FORMATION

Split Right (also called full, red). The running backs are split to both sides of the quarterback. The fullback is usually lined up to the strongside.

Split Right Formation (Full, Red)

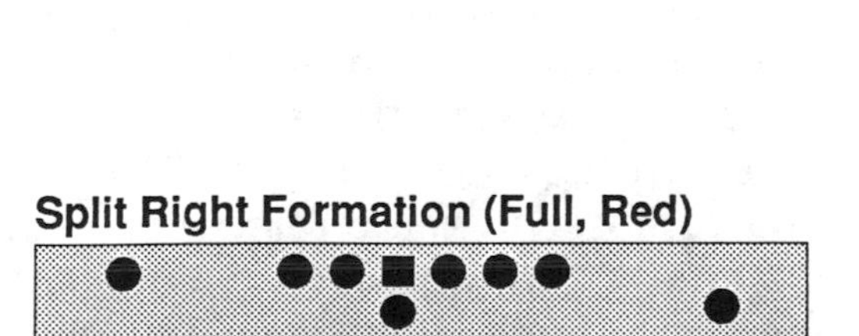

Far (also called opposite, brown). The fullback lines up behind the quarterback and the halfback is split to the weakside.

Far Formation (Opposite, Brown)

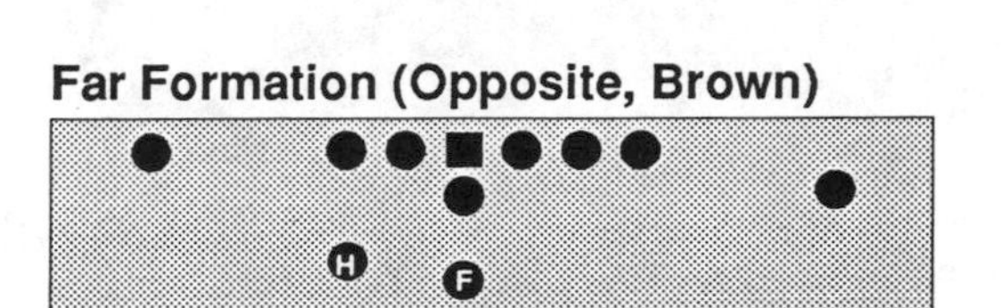

Near (also called blue, strong right). The fullback lines up behind the quarterback and the halfback is split to the strongside.

Near Formation (Blue, Strong Right)

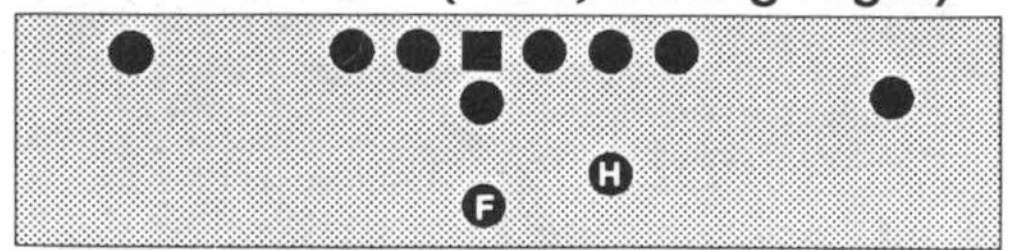

Green Bay Power Sweep. Vince Lombardi was a master at teaching running and blocking. He had a Hall of Fame running back tandem of Jim Taylor and Paul Hornung, who could both run and block, and linemen like Jerry Kramer and Fuzzy Thurston as the power blockers and pulling guards. The Green Bay Packers used the power sweep as often as a dozen times a game. Both guards pull to lead; the tight end blocks the outside linebacker, and the lead running back blocks the end. Look how similar Green Bay's power sweep, run out of the T-Formation variation called "Split Right," is to the single wing and the Notre Dame box. Note the offensive setup, called the pro set. It is the basic offensive formation today, with two wide receivers, one tight end, and two running backs.

Green Bay Power Sweep

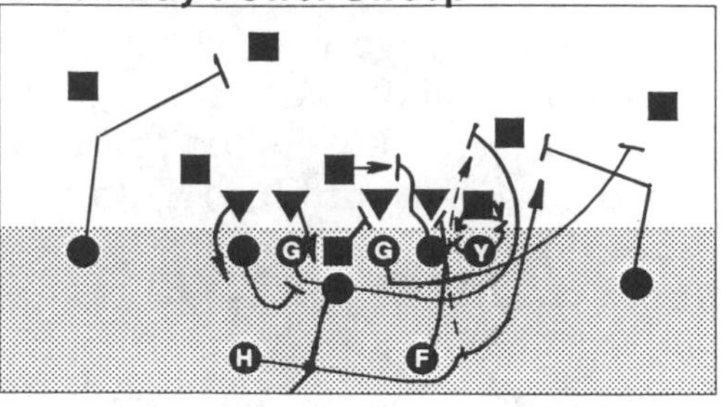

The Green Bay Packer Power Sweep.

I-FORMATION

The I-formation was invented in the 1950s by an obscure college coach named Tom Nugent. Hank Stram, who coached the Kansas City Chiefs to two of the first four Super Bowl games, was one of the first to use it in pro football. In the early 1970s other teams quickly copied the Chiefs' success. Stram often put his tight end in the I. The ballcarrier sets up deep, which allows him to "read" the blocks ahead of him and pick the hole he wants to run to. The I was Earl Campbell's trademark with the Houston Oilers, and then became Eric Dickerson's favorite formation with the Indianapolis Colts. A wide variety of fakes can be used in the I because the ball is screened until the last second. This formation is particularly effective on running plays up the middle or off tackle.

I-formation

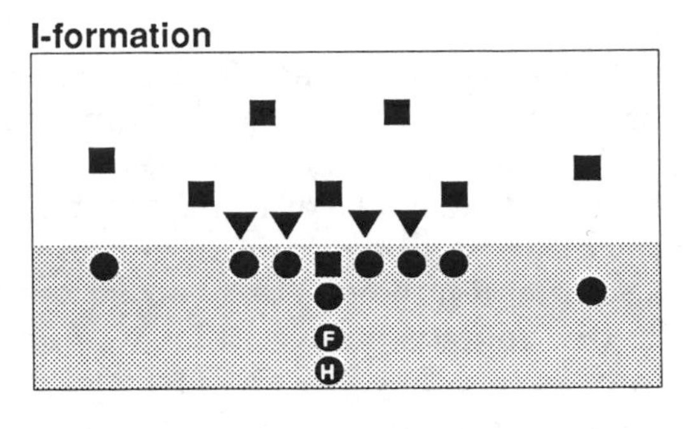

SHOTGUN

The shotgun was designed for the passing game, but not all teams use it. The Dallas Cowboys started using it in 1975 and won the NFC championship that season. Rather than taking the snap direct from the center, the quarterback sets up about four yards behind the center. This allows him to see more of the field and gives him more time to read the zones because he doesn't have to drop back.

Shotgun

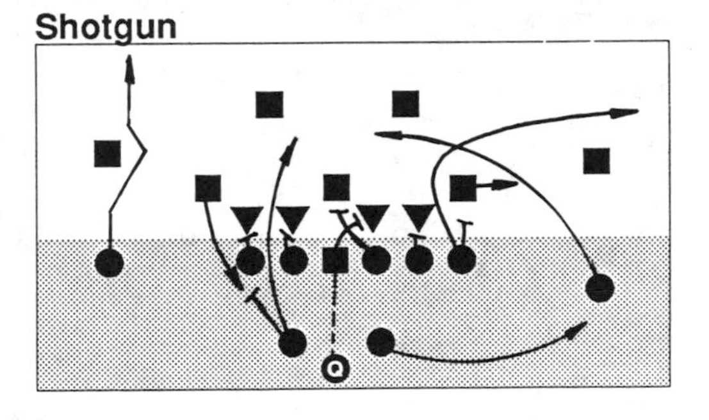

ONE-BACK OFFENSE

The one-back offense, devised in the last decade, uses two tight ends and only one running back. The second tight end is usually called the H-back, and is in a sense a relocated fullback. The advantages are: There is no weakside of the field, another blocker is set closer to the line, and a second tight end instead of a back can get

One-back Offense

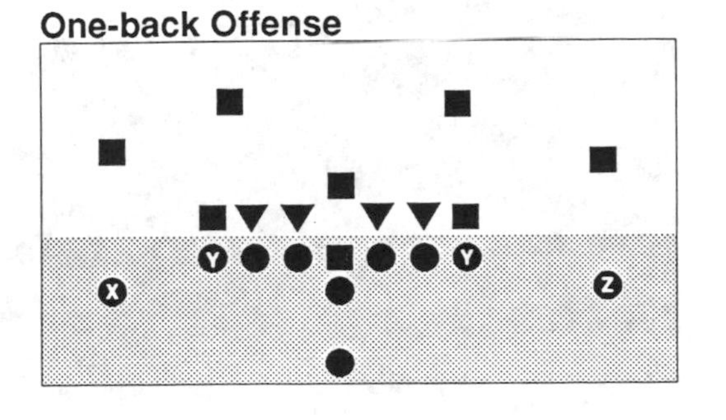

downfield quicker for passes. The one-back formation helps the running game by creating better running lanes, since the four receivers stretch the defense across the field.

The Washington Redskins went to the one-back offense in 1981 (Joe Gibbs's first season as head coach), and won the Super Bowl the next year. By 1983, more than half of the teams were using this formation, and now every team uses it on occasion.

Washington likes to put both tight ends on one side of the ball and both wide receivers on the other side. Then the Redskins send a running play toward the wide receivers, even though they are not as good blockers as the tight ends. Why? The defense has matched wide receivers with cornerbacks, who don't tackle as well as linebackers or safeties.

If the second tight end is lined up next to the tackle, it is a variation of the old T-formation. (The halfbacks have moved outside to become wide receivers.) If the tight end is away from the tackle, it is a variation of the I-formation. (The blocking back has moved out from behind the quarterback to where he is a receiver.)

MULTIPLE RECEIVER FORMATIONS

Many teams now use three or four wide receivers in passing situations, substituting for slower tight ends and running backs. You will sometimes see teams with no backs in the backfield. If there are three or four wide receivers, someone should be able to get open every time if the quarterback has time to get the ball off.

Every team has pretty much the same plays. Coaches just call them by different names. When a coach talks about his "system," he is really just talking about how he names his formations. Take the example of three great coaches: Paul Brown and Sid Gillman, who are already in the Pro Football Hall of Fame, and Tom Landry, who will be soon. When the running backs were split behind the quarterback and the fullback was on the same side as the tight end, Brown called it split right, Gillman called it full, and Landry called it red.

If the backs were split behind the quarterback and the halfback was on the same side as the tight end, Brown called it split left, Gillman called it half, and Landry called it green.

If the backs were not split but the full-

Four Wide Receiver Offense

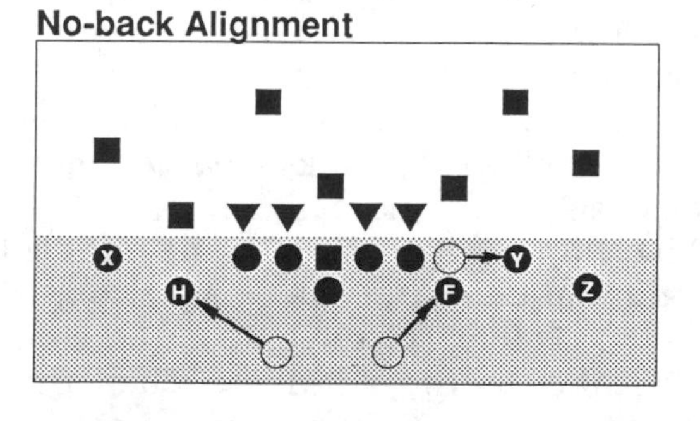

No-back Alignment

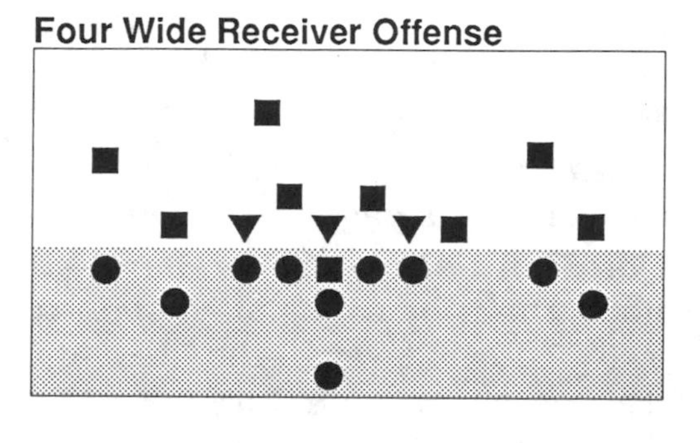

back was behind the quarterback and the halfback was opposite the tight end, Brown called it opposite, Gillman called it far, and Landry called it brown.

And if the fullback was in the same place but the halfback was on the same side as the tight end, Brown called it wing, Gillman called it near, and Landry called it blue.

Here's what determines what play is called. Coaches refer to it as down-and-distance.

First down. First down is either a running or a passing down. Many teams always run on first down at the beginning of the game. But they want to mix it up during the game. Teams want to be successful on first down, picking up four or five yards. Then there will be fewer yards to gain on the later downs. They can go for a big play on second down if they get eight or nine yards on first down.

Second-and-long or third-and-long. When five or more yards are needed, second and third are passing downs. Teams substitute players who are versatile, such as a running back who is an especially good receiver. More wide receivers and fewer tight ends and running backs will be used. Meanwhile, the defense substitutes more defensive backs for linebackers and linemen.

Second-and-four. Second-and-four can be either a run or a pass.

Second-and-short. Second-and-short is a good time for a big play, such as a bomb. If it doesn't work, the offense can pick up the first down on third down.

Third-and-short. Third down is a running down when the yardage needed is short. Teams will use two or three tight ends and fewer wide receivers, and bigger backs. The defense takes out defensive backs and puts in more linemen.

The running play called in the huddle is a combination of the basic formation, the man who is to carry the ball, and the hole in the line. In the old days, when there were four players in the backfield, the quarterback was number 1, the two halfbacks were numbers 2 and 4, and the fullback was number 3. Today, since there are only one or two running backs, they are numbered by the space they are set in, regardless of whether they are halfbacks or fullbacks—2 to the left, 3 behind the quarterback, and 4 to the right.

The second digit refers to the hole in the line. Odd numbers are usually to the left of the center and even numbers to the right.

Here's an example. We've already talked

The Holes and the Numbers

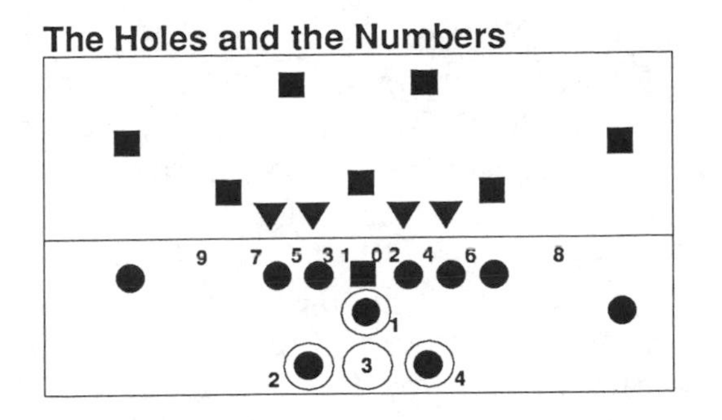

about the Green Bay Packers' famed power sweep. Today, the formation and play is usually called red right 38. Red right is the basic formation, with an end split out to the right and the backs split. The play is the 3 back—who is the fullback these days, lined up behind the quarterback—running into the 8 hole, around right end.

BLOCKING

Offensive linemen are the unsung heroes of football, the players who are rarely noticed unless they get called for a penalty or blow an assignment that causes a play to lose yardage. But they do a job just as important as anyone else on the field. Almost every time Eric Dickerson breaks a long run, or Joe Montana has time to pass, it's the offensive linemen who make the blocks that allow the play.

Pass blocking attempts to delay pass rushers charging across the line of scrimmage in "lanes," up the middle and from the sides. They want to pressure the quarterback from the front and squeeze him from the sides. And they have a variety of routes—through the blocker, past his inside shoulder or around his outside.

Blockers read the angle of the rush as they set up, trying to anticipate moves. In pass blocking, at the snap of the ball, offensive linemen stand and retreat to set up a "pocket" for the quarterback. When pass blocking, offensive linemen can use their hands as long as they do not reach out to grab a defender. In run blocking, offensive linemen "fire out" across the

Bengals lineman Anthony Munoz blocking.

line. They can extend their arms, but cannot hold defenders.

There are several kinds of blocking patterns.

Power Blocking is a straight-ahead, man-on-man attempt to push the defense back, with no attempt to deceive, double-team, or create a hole by concentrating on one area of the line. Defensive teams with quick but undersized linemen, like the Denver Broncos of the mid-1980s, are vulnerable to this approach.

Power Blocking

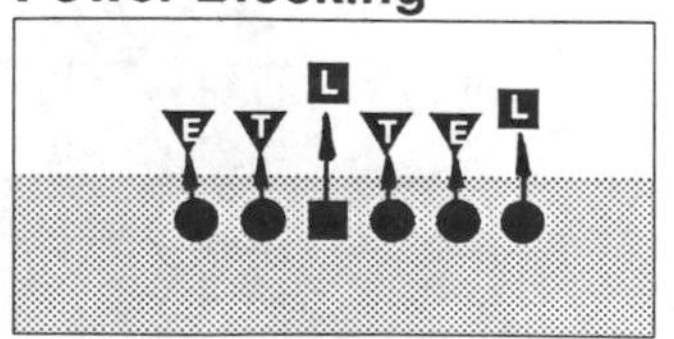

Angle Blocking is designed to create a "misdirection" play in which the blockers go one way but the ballcarrier—or, more likely, the quarterback on a partial rollout—gets the benefit of an extra step of maneuverability before the defense recovers.

Angle Blocking

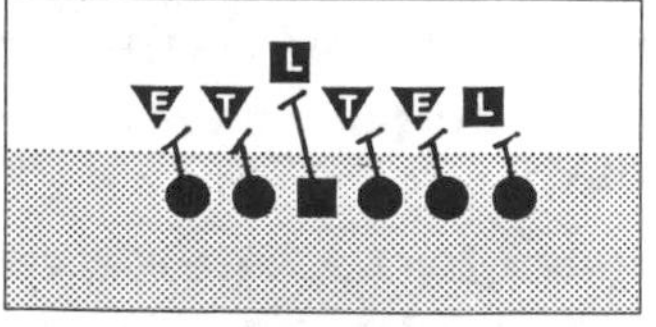

Double-Team Blocking is directed against a particularly talented defender who is consistently beating his assigned blocker, particularly in pass protection.

Double Team Blocking

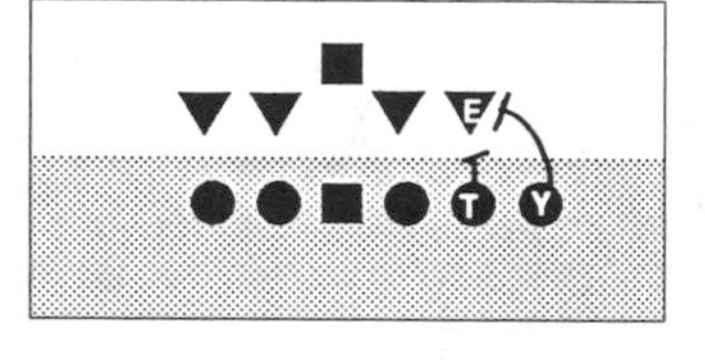

Wedge blocking is an attempt to overpower the defense at the point of attack, and is a simple "numbers game" approach to run blocking that goes back to football's earliest days.

Wedge Blocking

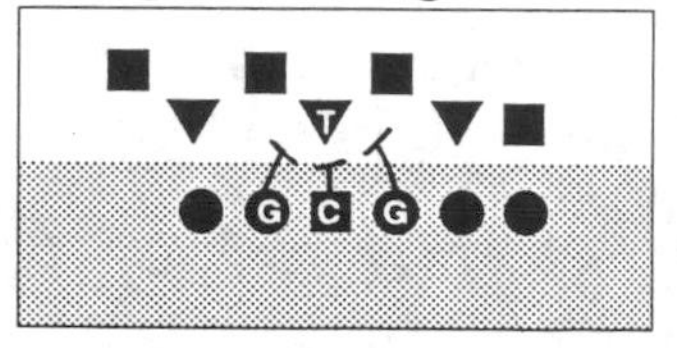

Cross blocking, also called scissors blocking, involves a switch of blocking assignments by two linemen. Cutting the defender down from the side just as he thinks he has a clear path toward the ballcarrier or quarterback will slow his forward rush next time.

Cross Blocking

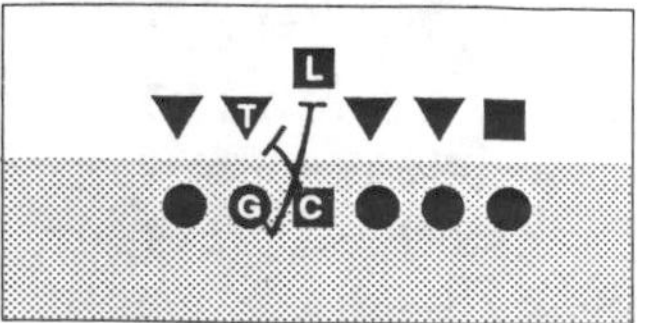

Lead blocking involves timing the handoff so that one of the backs can follow a lineman into the designated hole, to be followed by the ballcarrier. If the blocking back is not tangled up with a defensive lineman, he continues through the line to block the linebacker, with his running mate following for perhaps a big gain.

Isolation Blocking is a delay in blocking a man who is unchecked at the line. This is no accident; the play calls for the ball to go elsewhere while the defender is rushing madly ahead.

Lead Blocking

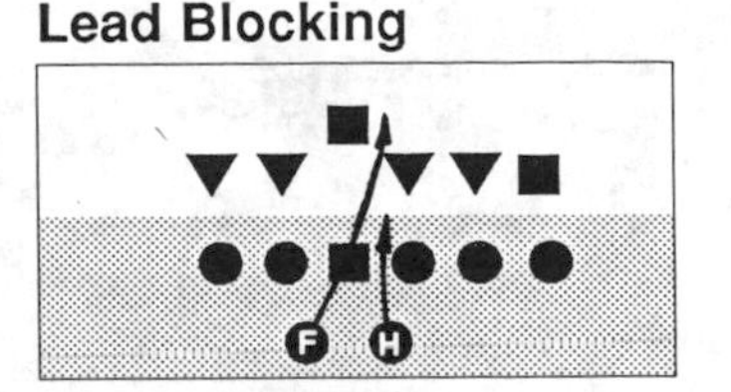

Isolation Blocking

THE PASSING TREE

Since different pass patterns are required for wide receivers, tight ends and running backs, every team has what is called a passing tree. When drawn on a blackboard, a typical passing diagram looks like a leafless tree, with every branch a numbered pass route. The odd numbers are the outside routes and the even numbers are the inside routes.

On every play, the receiver needs to know the formation (where he lines up), the snap count (when he releases), and a single digit number (the route he runs). The X receiver's route is the first number called, the Y tight end is the second number, and the Z receiver is the third. Thus, on a "976," for example, the split end runs an up (straight up the field), the tight end does a deep corner, and the flanker runs in. Some teams use only a two-digit play call, depending on whether the wide receiver or the tight end is the primary receiver.

Just as a quarterback reads a certain key or keys as he is setting up, the receiver has keys to read on some patterns to tell him if he is to break the route into a specific area or to run away from the coverage. True coordination between the quarterback and his receivers occurs when they read the same thing and are in a situation where they know beforehand to whom the pass will be thrown.

Passing Tree — Wide Receivers

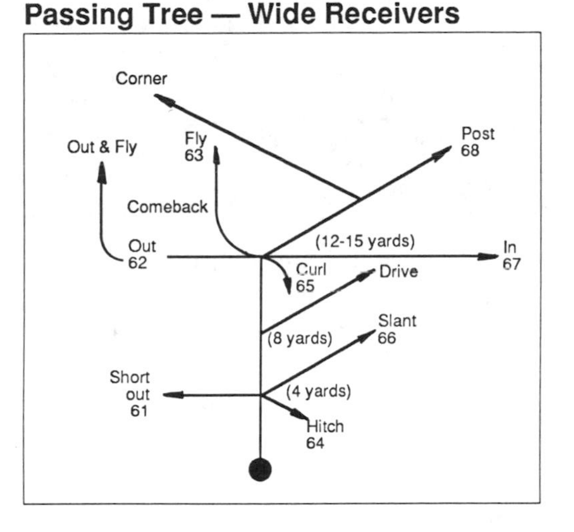

Passing Tree — Tight Ends

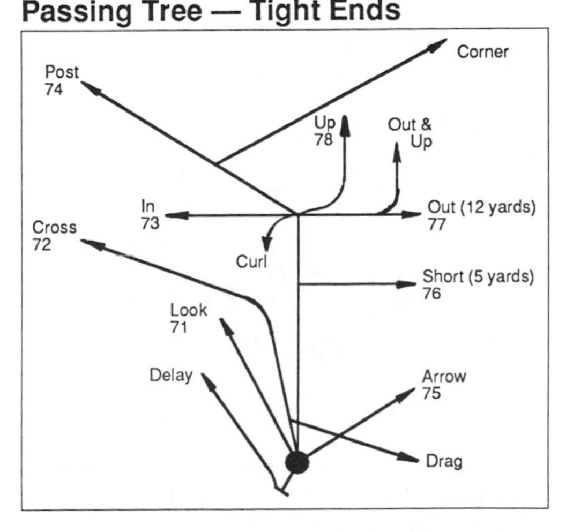

Thus, every pass pattern has a contingency—a set of automatic adjustments, or breakoffs—for the receivers. For example, if the defensive back plays one way, the receiver breaks off the pattern and goes to the option.

Here are some of the most common pass routes.

Slant. The slant is used when the defensive back is playing off the line. The receiver charges out, takes two or three steps, then cuts to the middle, in front of the defender.

Quick out. As with the slant, in the quick out the receiver takes a couple of steps, then cuts to the sidelines.

Out. On an out, the receiver breaks toward the sidelines at an angle, coming back toward the line of scrimmage. That keeps the defender from being able to get to the ball.

Curl. A curl—coming back to the line of scrimmage—is the easiest way to catch the ball.

Post. To execute a post, the receiver breaks to the defensive back's inside shoulder, as with a curl, gets him going the wrong way, then cuts upfield toward the goalpost.

Fly. For a fly, the receiver gives the defensive back a quick stutter step, as though running a post, then goes straight upfield.

Corner. To do a corner, the receiver does the stem, then the post for five or six yards, then breaks to the corner.

Running backs also have a passing tree, and they have breakoff patterns.

Breakoff Patterns

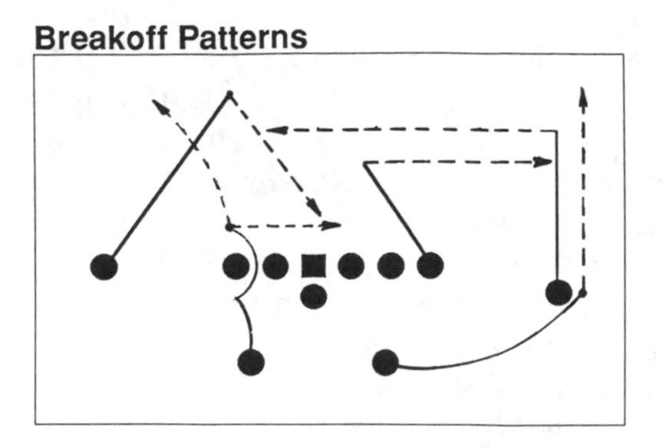

Passing Tree — Running Backs

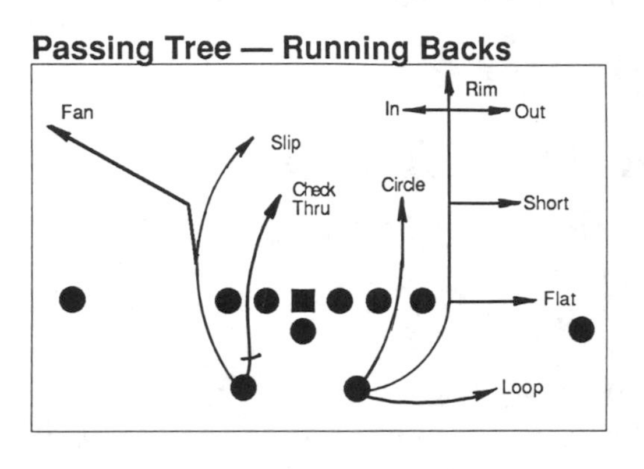

AUDIBLES

Audibles are also called automatics or checkoffs. Plays are usually called by the coaches nowadays, but quarterbacks almost always have the freedom to call an audible. Just before the quarterback is going to yell "hut," if he sees something in the defense (that's called reading the defense), such as a safety blitz, that causes him to change the play, he will call an audible. Audibles start with a "live" color or number, a predetermined code that alerts the team to a new play. The code is quickly followed by a new play number. During this time, a quarterback will be looking not at his receivers (because he already knows what they will be doing), but at the defense and how it reacts at the snap of the ball.

An audible can be either protective or aggressive. It can protect an offense from wasting a play if the defense is aligned in a way that will successfully counter the play called in the huddle, or it can take advantage of an unexpected weakness in the defensive alignment. Half the big plays in a game are from audibles, say some coaches.

Here are some examples of when to call an audible: The weakside linebacker looks as if he's going to blitz, so a halfback draw to that side might go all the way; or the defensive right end isn't crashing to the inside and can be blocked outside, so the offense might run a slant outside tackle. Or, if the offense is planning a sweep to the right but the defense is strong there, the offense might switch to a play going to the weakside.

But, remember, defenses try to disguise their formations so the offense can't guess their plan. A defensive back might move into one position to pretend he's going to be in man-to-man coverage and then jump into a different area when the quarterback is in the middle of calling out his signals. It often turns into a guessing game—with the team that does the best guessing coming up the winner more often than not.

Remember, reading the defense, not play-calling, is the best measure of a quarterback's intellect in today's game.

SITUATIONAL SUBSTITUTION

In the old days, 11 men played both ways in football, meaning they played both offense and defense for 60 minutes. That started to change in the 1950s when the first full-time defensive players began to appear. By the 1960s, placekickers and punters became specialized jobs.

Today, while there are still 11 starters on both offense and defense, anywhere from one to several players run on and off the field depending on down and distance. That's called situational substitution or specialization. Years ago, running backs were asked to run, catch, and block. Today, the best runner plays in running situations and the best pass catcher plays in pass situations. Substitution gets more specialized players into the game, such as a pass-rushing defensive end or a running back who is a very good pass receiver.

For example, on offense, if a team is stopped for a loss on first down, it might go immediately to its passing offense, putting in extra wide receivers and taking out a running back and the tight end. Or on a third-down play when only a foot is needed for a first down, two big backs might come in along with two or three tight ends, with smaller players going out. There is even more substitution on defense, with five, six, or seven defensive backs replacing linemen and linebackers in passing situations, and extra defensive linemen playing on running downs.

Offenses sometimes play without huddles to keep defenses from substituting (with the quarterback calling plays at the line of scrimmage). But the more a team substitutes, the more it risks confusing its players. You often see timeouts in these situations because there might be only 10 players on the field. Or a penalty is called when there are 12 men on the field.

Situational substitution doesn't mean a team is going to succeed on the play; it just means it is in a better position to do so.

BEATING THE BLITZ

When a blitz by the defense is imminent, the quarterback and his receivers must alter their play to complete a pass before the quarterback is sacked. Each receiver has to read the blitz and make a move in response, usually shortening his route or making a quick break to the outside.

The best way to stop the blitz is by having a running back stay in to block or by pulling a left guard to pick up a linebacker.

Here are a few examples of how to beat the weakside linebacker blitzing on third-and-long: a flare pass to the halfback on the weakside, a screen pass to the weakside, and a down-and-in pass to the tight end coming across. All these plays take advantage of the weakside linebacker's having vacated his normal position in order to penetrate the line. Here's a diagram of how to beat a full blitz with a screen pass to a fullback.

Play Action Pass

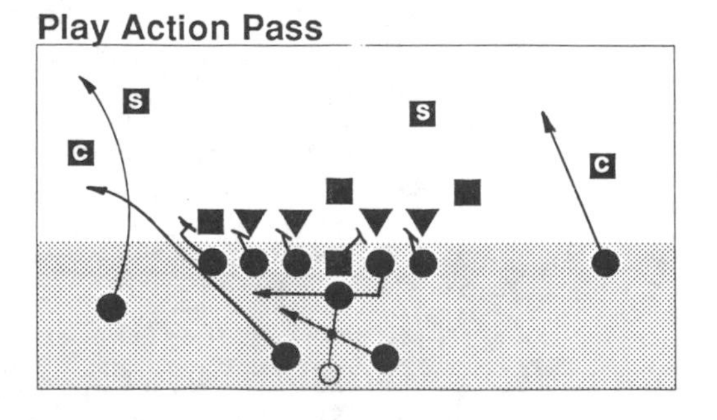

TWO-MINUTE OFFENSE

One of the most dramatic moments in sports occurs when a team is fighting the clock and the opponent as it drives downfield in the final two minutes of a game. The two-minute drill is one of those misnomers of football—it often lasts 15 minutes or more. But it is the time of the game in which great quarterbacks and great teams are at their best. Hall of Famers Johnny Unitas, Bobby Layne, and Roger Staubach (who supposedly won 14 games in the final two minutes) were some of the masters of the two-minute offense. More recently, Denver's quarterback John Elway will always be known for "the drive,"

The Dallas Cowboys make a goal line stand.

a 98-yard drive he led in the 1986 NFL championship game to defeat the Cleveland Browns and send the Broncos to the Super Bowl.

What is needed most in the final two minutes is an attitude of total disbelief that you are going to lose. Players cannot even think about losing the game. Execution is all that matters. During this time, the advantage is with the offense. The team with the ball knows the plays and what the defense will do. Most of the pass plays are short and hard to defend, usually sideline patterns that get the receiver out of bounds and stop the clock. It's easy to get in 10 plays in the final two minutes of a game if you use the clock wisely, whereas you might have only four plays in a two-minute span earlier in the game.

Offensive plays are designed to strike deep, medium, or short, depending on what the defense will give up and what the offense has to do to conserve time on the clock. Some of the best pass plays during the final two minutes of a game or a half are quick passes, strongside "floods"—plays that flood one area of the field with receivers—weakside floods, deep floods, fullback screen, and halfback delay. (See glossary for more on these plays.) Running plays in the two-minute drill are designed and executed with one thing in mind—gaining the maximum yards possible while making good use of the sidelines to stop the clock. A quick trap and a quick toss are both good running plays.

GOAL-LINE OFFENSE

When a team gets inside the 10-yard line, it wants to score a touchdown, or at least come away with a field goal. The last thing it wants to do is turn over the ball. Near the goal line is no place to get fancy.

Most goal-line offenses bring in an extra tight end to replace a wide receiver, making the formation strong on both sides. That also creates eight running holes, or gaps, that the defense has to cover. One popular goal-line play is the quick trap, designed to split two defensive linemen. Vince Lombardi said the Green Bay Packers scored 16 touchdowns one season by using the quick trap. An off-tackle run is also a good play to call.

If a team is going to pass, a rollout is a favorite with a mobile quarterback. The wide receiver takes the cornerback deep and the fullback flares to the sideline. The quarterback then runs or passes, depending on whether the safety commits for the pass or comes up for the run.

Here are two versions of goal-line pass plays: In the first, the quarterback rolls right behind the halfback (who was slotted left) and the fullback. The "Z" receiver runs to the inside, then cuts to the sideline just before the goal line. The pass should be thrown just as he makes his cut.

In the second diagram, again going to the right, the offense floods the right side of the end zone with three receivers. The "X" and "Z" receivers first go in motion to the left before cutting outside. The quarterback rolls slightly to the right, trying to loft a pass to the "X" receiver.

Goal-line Offense (No. 1)

Goal-line Offense (No. 2)

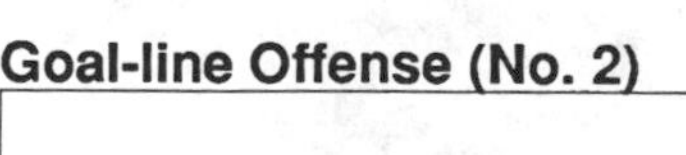

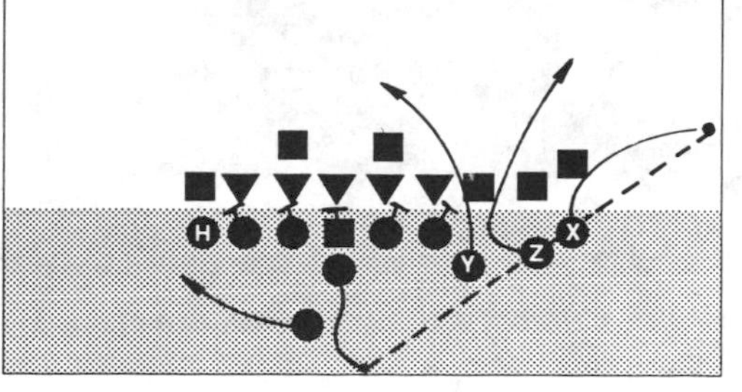

GIMMICKS AND GADGETS

Every team has tricks up its sleeves, but you'll see them more in college football than in the pros. The most common are reverses, the halfback option (either run or pass), a flea-flicker play, a pass to a quarterback, the end-around, the tackle-eligible, or a fake punt.

"People want to play it safe," said Bill Walsh, who coached the San Francisco 49ers to three Super Bowl championships in the 1980s. "The conservative approach won't cost anybody his job."

But gimmick plays are being used more often. If teams run the same plays every time, it's easy for a defense to get ready. You want your offense to be unpredictable. Even if a gimmick play doesn't work, it makes the defense think, "What if they try it again?"

CHAPTER THREE

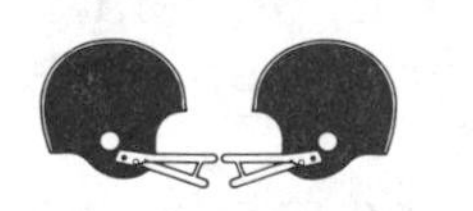

The Plays

RUNNING PLAYS

Many different running plays are used in football. We'll discuss the ones used the most. Remember, however, that during a game you'll want to mix your ballcarriers and blocking styles. Keeping the defense off-balance is as important for a good running game as it is for the passing game.

Sweep. In the sweep, the ballcarrier takes a handoff from the quarterback and runs parallel to the line of scrimmage while allowing his blockers (the guards and sometimes a tackle) to get in front before he turns the corner. It is aimed at the defensive end, the outside linebacker, and the cornerback who comes up to force the play. It is more difficult to run the sweep against a 3–4 defense. The play is set up by the other running back's faking into the line and looking to block a defensive lineman.

Green Bay Packer Hall of Fame running back Jim Taylor turns the corner.

Sweep

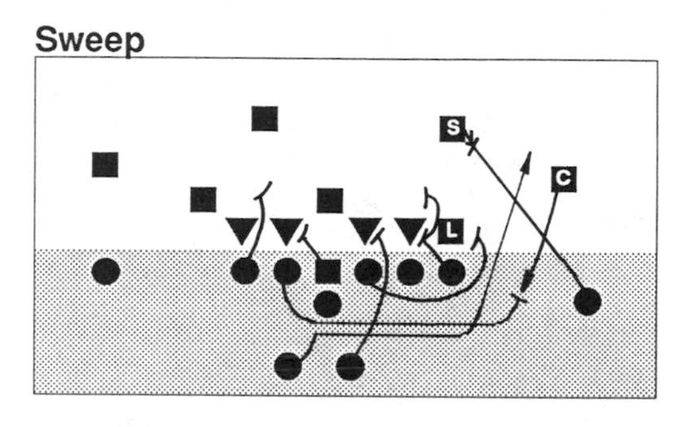

Dive. Every team has a play like the dive. The running back takes a quick handoff and hits the hole between tackle and guard. He often has the other running back out in front, with the middle linebacker as his target.

Dive

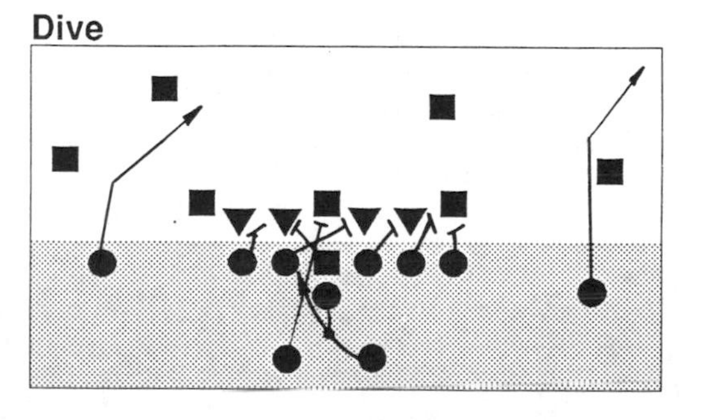

Pitch. The pitch involves the quarterback's faking the ball to one running back who heads up the middle, then tossing a short lateral to the other set back who has begun his move to the outside.

Pitch

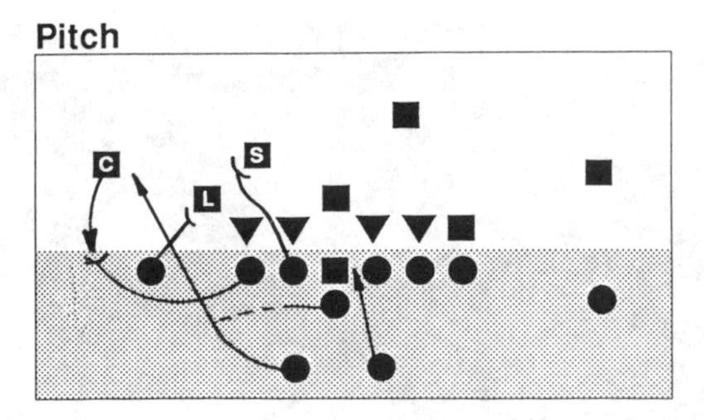

Veer. The veer is another quick-hitting play, where the ball can be handed off to either back, whose route is determined by the reaction of the defensive linemen.

Veer

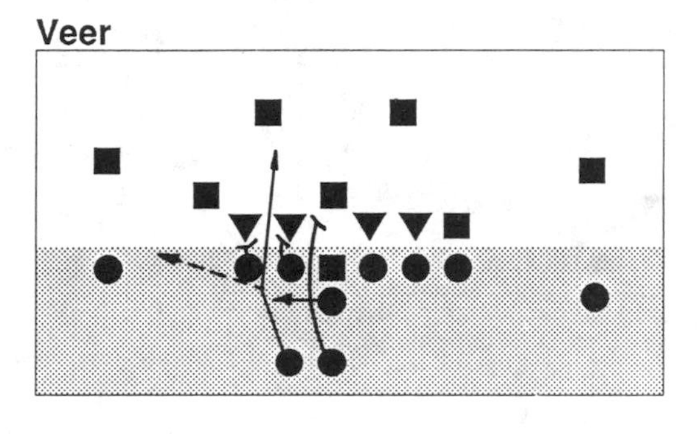

Slant. In the slant, the running back runs at an angle, or slant, toward the hole. The other back also runs at that same angle to lead interference.

Slant

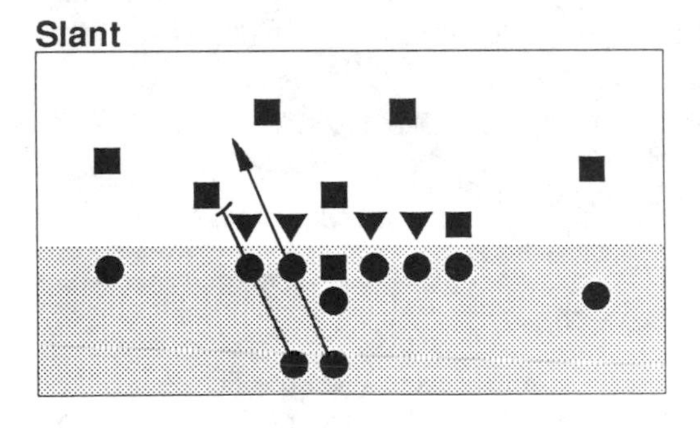

Draw. The draw begins as a simulated pass, like a screen, then suddenly develops into a run. The offensive linemen retreat, just as if they are pass blocking, inviting the defense to charge. The quarterback drops back too, almost to normal passing depth. Then he suddenly turns and hands the ball off to a running back. The defensive linemen, in their anxiety to rush the quarterback, may leave a fairly big unprotected area at the line of scrimmage. As the running back bursts toward the line, the offensive linemen turn the rushers to the side. A draw is the opposite of play-action, because the offensive players act as if the play is a pass, and it turns into a run.

Draw

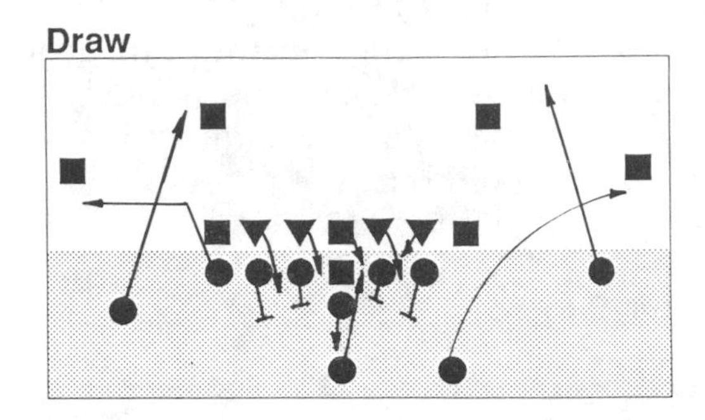

Baltimore Colt Hall of Famers Johnny Unitas (top) and Alan Ameche (bottom).

Trap. The trap is football's best sucker play. It takes advantage of the enthusiastic or reckless charge of a defensive lineman and turns his quick reactions against him. To trap this player, a guard vacates his normal blocking area and allows the defensive lineman to penetrate the line so he has a clear shot to the backfield. Then he is blocked out by the guard from the opposite side, who pulls and hits him from the side. The ballcarrier cuts behind the trap block. If the defender is taken by surprise and blocked out, the offense can exploit the hole that is made.

Trap Play

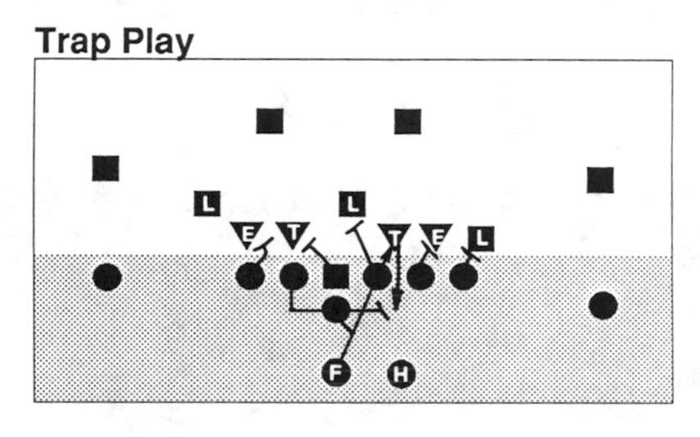

Buffalo Hall of Fame running back O. J. Simpson runs a trap against the Jets.

Long Trap. The long trap is run from shotgun formation and has an extra advantage because it comes from a passing formation on a passing down (note the three wide receivers). In this diagram, the pass-rushing defensive left end takes himself out of the play by going after the quarterback, which frees the offensive right tackle to help the ballcarrier farther downfield by blocking the strong safety. The defensive left tackle is the victim of the trap block.

Long Trap Play

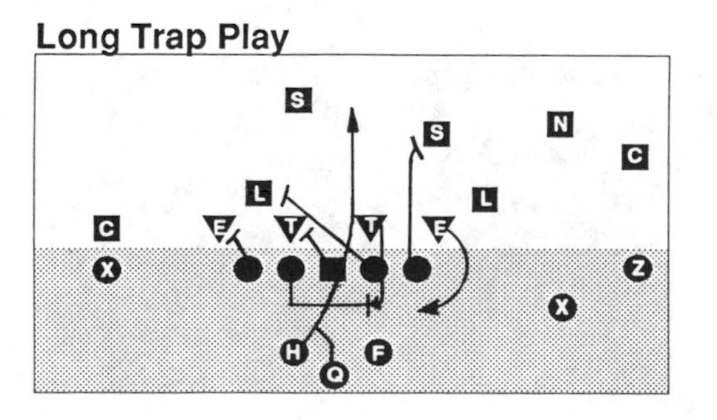

Off-Tackle. The off-tackle is one of the oldest plays in football, and is reminiscent of the days of the single wing. On this play, the running back dives through the hole opened by the blocks of the tight end, the pulling guard, and the fullback. The off-tackle attacks the defense where it is weakest—at the strongside linebacker.

Off-Tackle Play

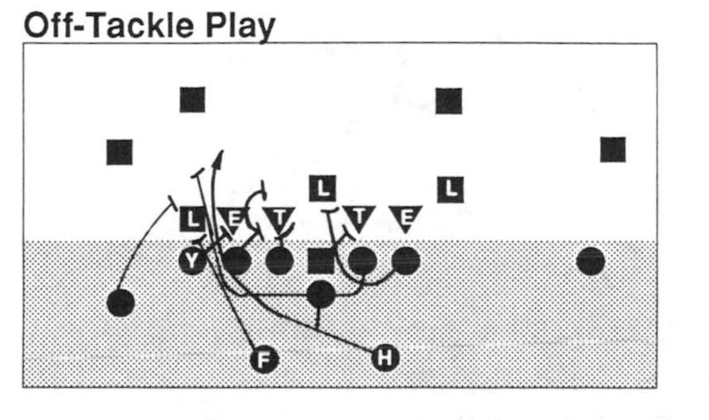

One-Back Run. Depending on the motion, the one-back run can be used from any of several formations. The blocks at the point of attack are very important, especially the left tackle on the defensive right end, the left guard needing some movement on the right inside linebacker, and the center cutting off the nose tackle. Notice the H-back, the second tight end, who blocks the weak outside linebacker to the outside. The running back has three lanes to choose from: over tackle, cut back over guard, or outside tackle.

One-Back Run

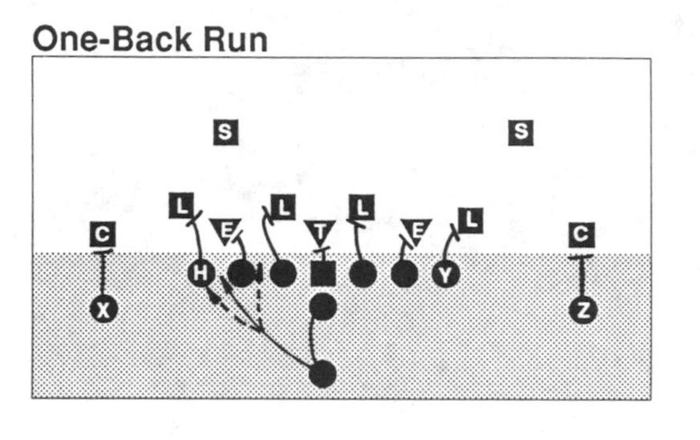

Counter Play (Misdirection). When a running play looks as if it is going in one direction and ends up going in another, it's called a counter. In the play diagrammed, the quarterback fakes a lateral to the halfback, who decoys around right end. The fullback takes a handoff and hits up the middle behind the center, who changes blocking assignments with the weakside guard.

Counter Play (Misdirection)

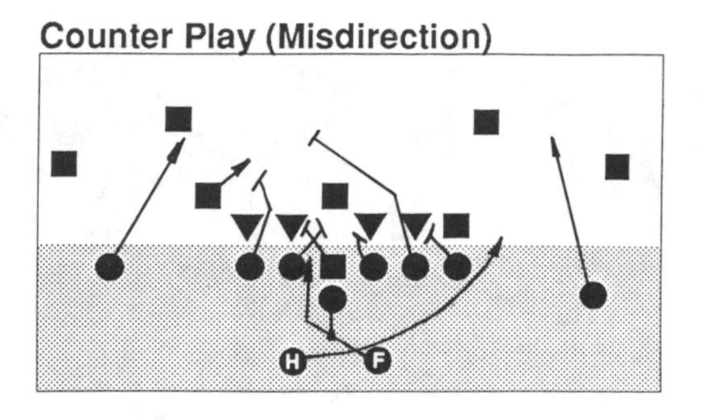

I-Formation Run. The I-formation run uses a tailback's power and quickness, especially if the block on the strong safety is accurately read and the outside lane opens up. On this play, the strongside guard pulls and blocks the strongside linebacker (S); the tight end (Y) and strongside tackle double-team the defensive end; the weakside guard assists with the block on the left inside linebacker; the center blocks the nose tackle; the fullback blocks the strong safety; the flanker takes the cornerback. Finally, the tailback takes the toss from the quarterback and reads the block by the strongside guard and the fullback's holding off the strong safety.

I-formation Run

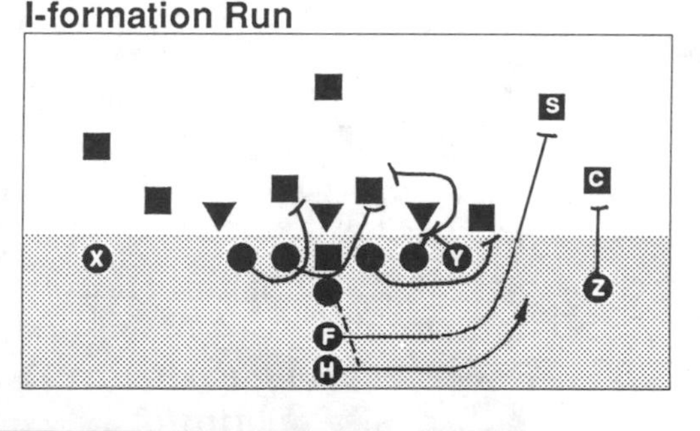

A Raider running back gets blocking up front.

Houston Oiler Hall of Famer Earl Campbell running from the I-formation.

Quarterback Sneak. When you need only a yard for a first down or a touchdown, the quarterback sneak is a popular play. It is almost impossible to stop before the needed yard is obtained. All it involves is the quarterback's taking the snap from center and following the straight-ahead blocking of his center and guards.

Quarterback Sneak

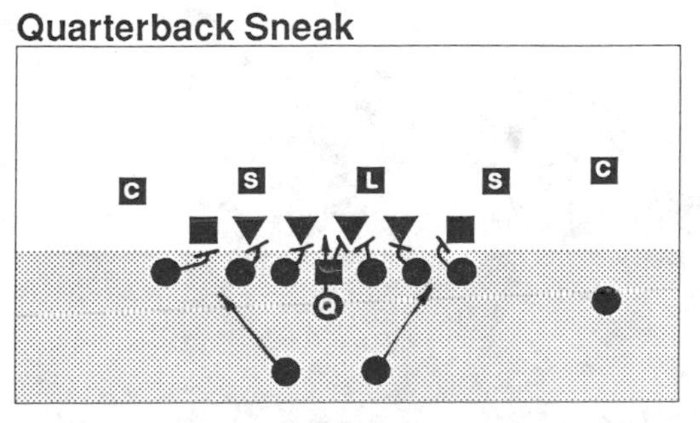

Quarterback Bootleg. The quarterback bootleg is rarely used anymore because coaches are afraid to use their high-salaried quarterbacks as ballcarriers. In the bootleg, the quarterback has the option of either running or passing, depending on what the defense does. On this weakside bootleg, the backs fake to the strongside and the quarterback fakes the ball to them. If the defense rushes the quarterback, he'll throw to a wide receiver who's usually running a square-out route or a turn-in route. If the linebacker drops back on the weakside, then the quarterback will run the ball. He usually has a blocker in front of him. In this diagram it is the pulling guard.

Quarterback Bootleg

PASS PLAYS

Most passes are thrown no more than 15 yards. The strategy on these short passes is to move running backs into certain areas to force linebackers to move accordingly—which often leaves a receiver uncovered. On longer passes, the receiver's job is basically simple—he just has to "get open." To do so, he uses a variety of moves and patterns to shake off his defender.

But the best way to attack a good pass defense is to use the whole field—spread it out with short, medium, and long passes.

Play Action. Play action is just like a backyard game where the quarterback says in the huddle, "I'm going to fake to you and throw a pass." The idea is to make the play look exactly like a run when it is really a pass. In this diagram, the quarterback fakes to the fullback before dropping back and throwing to one of two targets on the left, either the running back short or the wide receiver looping deep and toward the sideline. The pulling guard also helps to establish "run" in the minds of the defense, as do the rest of the linemen, who carry out their run-blocking assignments. It's the most widely used method of controlling the linebackers, because they either step forward to try to make a tackle that isn't there, or they freeze in their tracks for a second and are out of position to cover the pass that is about to be thrown.

Play Action Pass

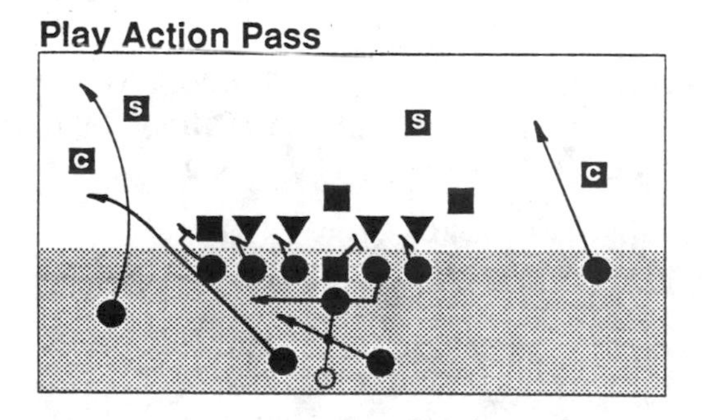

Screen Pass. The screen is used when the defense expects a pass. It works well against a zone defense because the linebackers have run off from their areas and are out of position to tackle the receiver. The quarterback drops to his regular passing position, and he wants the defense to drop back, particularly the linebackers. The offensive linemen set up as they would for a pass block, trying to get the defensive linemen to charge. The receivers run downfield, faking a deep pass. The backs set as they do on a pass. As the pass rushers hit the "pocket," the quarterback retreats a little deeper, then throws a pass out to a running back who has released his stance as a blocker and faded out into "the flat"—the unoccupied zone past the charging defenders and short of the retreating secondary.

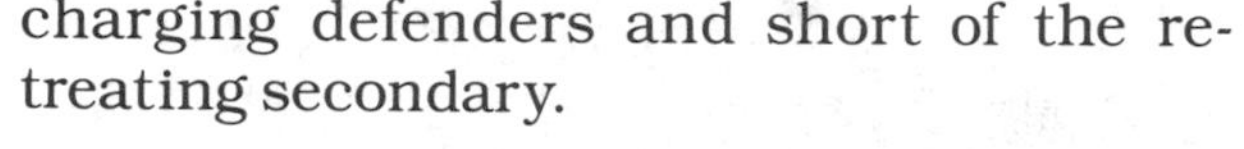

Screen Pass

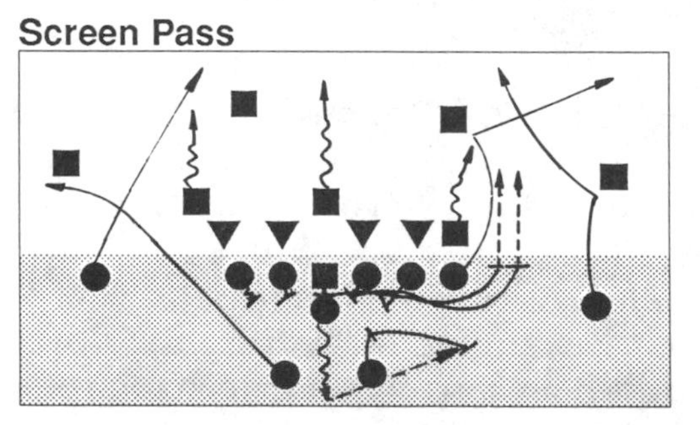

Dallas Cowboy Hall of Famer Roger Staubach demonstrates his passing prowess.

Option Screen Pass. On the option screen pass, the primary receiver is the flanker, who runs a quick route along the sideline. The quarterback either throws immediately to a spot ahead of the receiver or keeps the ball momentarily if the receiver is not open right away. Then the quarterback drops back into his "pocket" and waits for a normal screen pass to develop, which gives the secondary receiver a wall of blockers.

Option Screen Pass

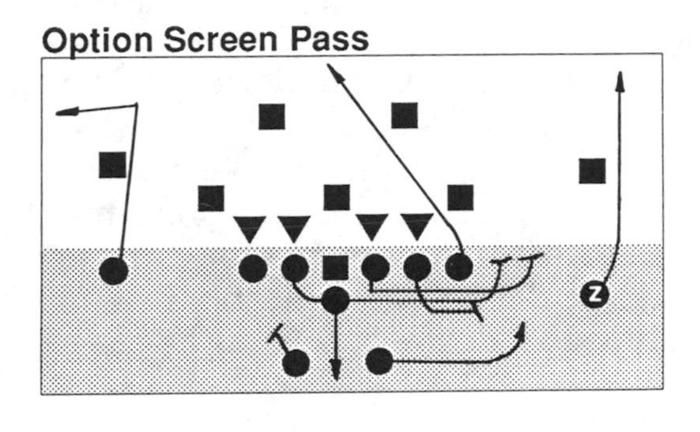

Rollout Pass. Rollout passes are a fine gainer if the wide receiver can get open. They get the quarterback out on the edge of the formation, giving him a good view of the field. (A waggle is the opposite of rolling out, setting up away from the flow.) In the first diagram, the quarterback rolls to his right behind the pulling center, while the halfback, slotted right, goes in motion left to draw some pressure off the quarterback. The "Z" receiver runs an out, trying to keep the cornerback inside. In the second diagram, the tight end is the intended receiver.

Rollout Pass (No. 1)

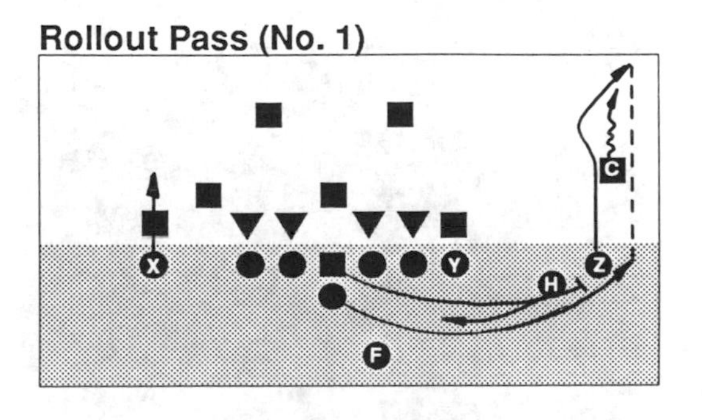

Rollout Pass (No. 2)

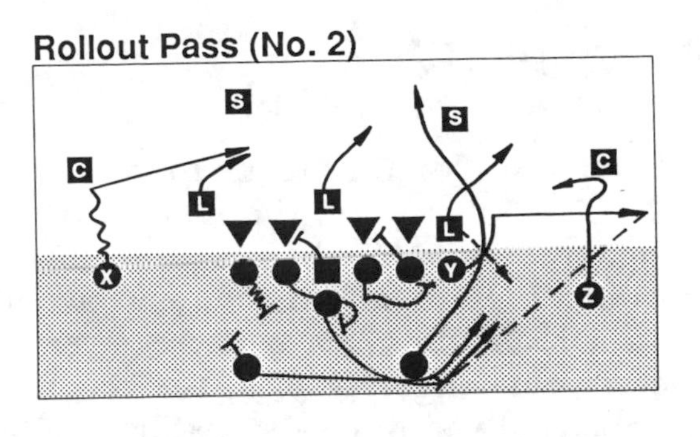

Deep Flood. Nothing is more spectacular, and nothing puts points up on the scoreboard faster than the bomb. But the passing game is more than the bomb. It consists of intelligent route running, the ability to read the defenses, and the courage to hold the ball in the pocket until the right moment. The quarterback takes a seven-step drop, while the receivers normally fake a pattern, then go deep, flooding the secondary.

Deep Flood

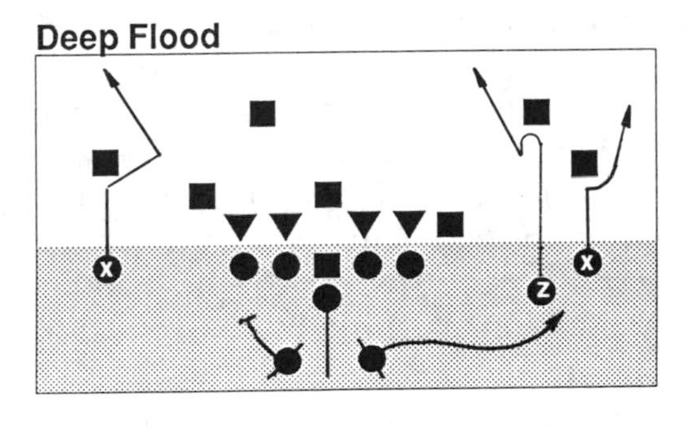

Inside Deep. One way to beat a zone defense is to flood one of the zones with several receivers. In the inside deep play, the Y receiver (tight end) does a down-and-in in front of the weak safety, the Z flanker runs a deeper down-and-in away from the cornerback, and the X receiver goes deep on a fly route. The outlet receivers are the halfback and fullback running flare patterns to the outside.

Inside Deep Pass

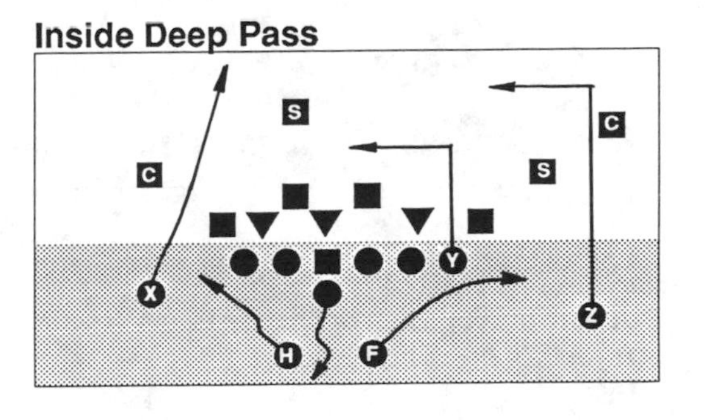

Combination. In combination patterns, the team tries to use all the receivers to strike deep, medium, and short at the same time. The quarterback takes a seven-step drop and looks for an open receiver.

Combination Pass

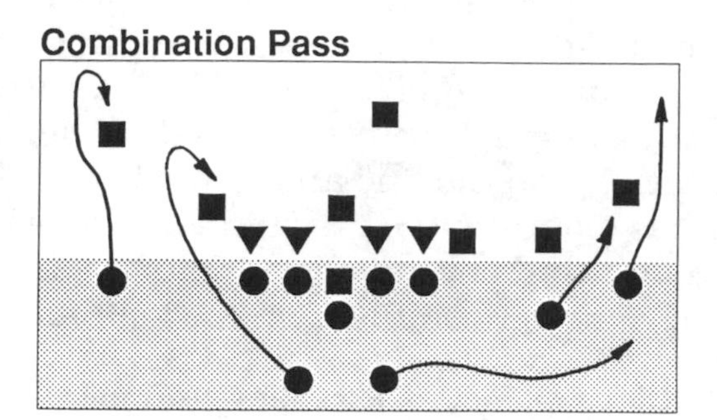

Tight End As a Receiver. In today's game, the tight end is being used more and more as a receiving threat, especially on long passes. One of the biggest plays is a tight end running deep between the two zones in a two-deep zone defense. In the diagram, the tight end, the primary receiver, runs a corner route.

Tight End as a Receiver

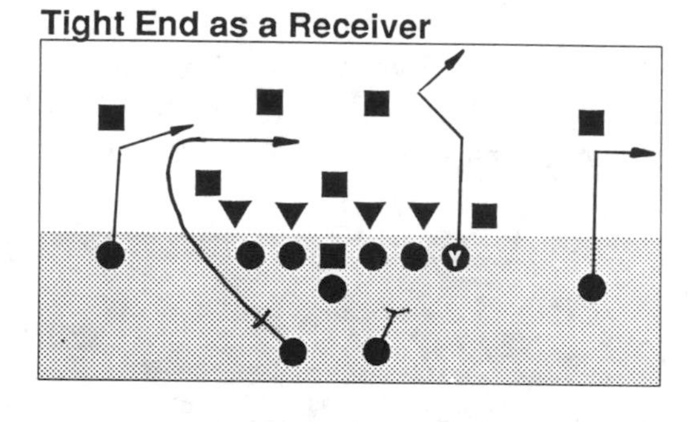

Short Passing Game. Offenses want to maintain ball control, and they can do that by passing short. The short game sends out wide receivers as decoys to draw defensive backs away from the line of scrimmage, then it floods the running backs and tight ends with high-percentage passes, most traveling no more than 10 yards beyond the line of scrimmage. Many teams, such as the Minnesota Vikings, use a short passing game that features a running back as a frequent receiver after the wide receivers have cleared out his short area by running longer routes. San Francisco coach George Seifert is one of the leading advocates of a short passing game. The 49ers like to feature wide receivers as primary targets in a short passing game by running crossing routes while a running back and tight end go farther downfield.

Short Passing Game — Vikings

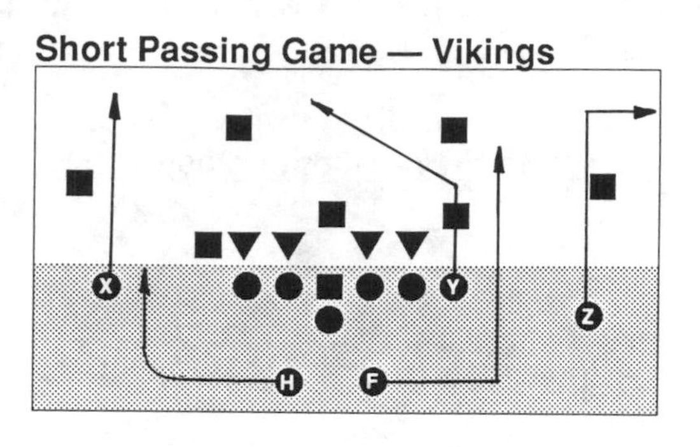

Short Passing Game — 49ers

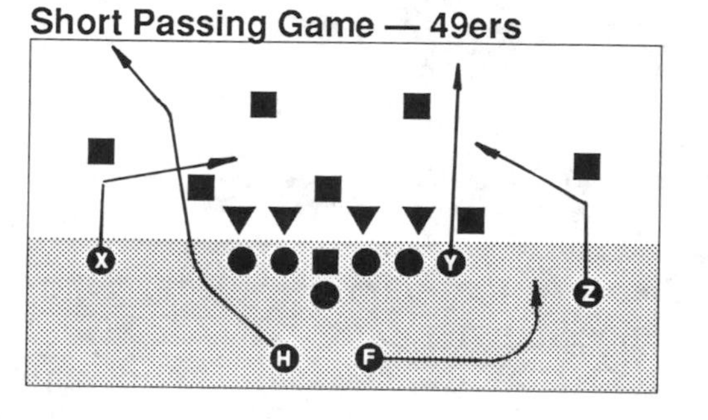

Deception—Halfback Option. Halfback option passes are passes by a running back, who can either run or pass; it's his option. Walter Payton, the NFL's all-time leading rusher, threw eight touchdown passes during his career. Option passes put a great deal of pressure on linebackers and the defensive backs. Halfback option passes are usually thrown from a sweep. In this diagram, the option is by the fullback.

Deception Play — Option Pass

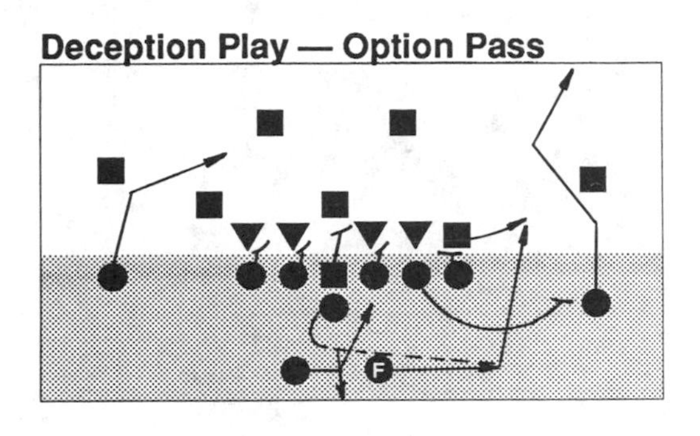

GIMMICK PLAYS

Flea-Flicker. The flea-flicker is one of the most entertaining plays to watch in football. The quarterback, who usually lines up in the shotgun, takes the snap and makes a short lateral to the lone running back, who heads toward the strongside behind the pulling weak tackle. Before he turns the corner, the halfback stops, pivots, and passes to the quarterback, who has run into the left flat while the defense shifts toward the expected run. In other variations of the flea-flicker, the halfback almost immediately laterals back to the quarterback, who throws to a wide receiver in a post pattern.

Gimmick Play — Flea-Flicker

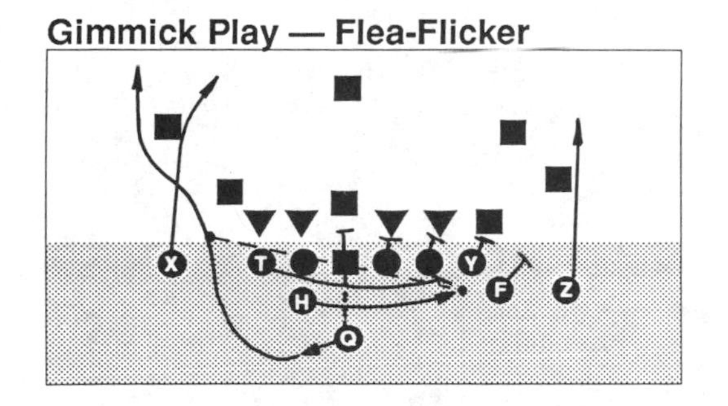

Turmoil Play. The turmoil play was a favorite of the Washington Redskins when Joe Theismann quarterbacked them to Super Bowls XVII and XVIII. Through a combination of shifts and motion before the snap, the running backs, tight ends, and wide receivers all move in predetermined different directions. Anything can come out of the chaos, which often frees the quarterback and confuses the defense, especially on the line and in the backfield. In this diagram, the quarterback drops behind all the movement and lofts a pass to the X receiver coming from the left flank.

Gimmick Play — Redskins' Turmoil

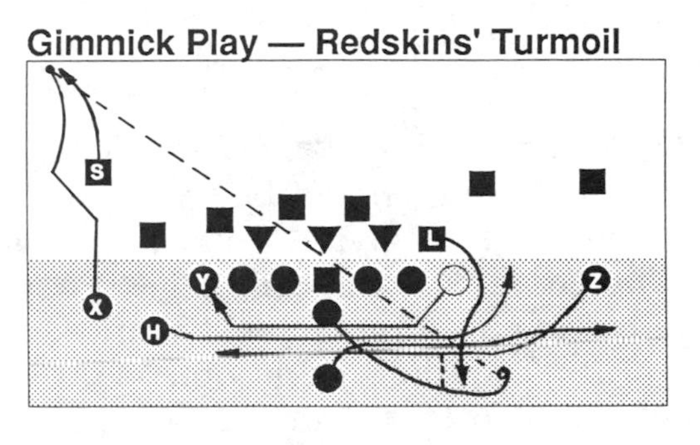

End Reverse and Fake Reverse. The Green Bay Packers used to work end reverse and fake reverse plays to perfection with James Lofton, one of the quickest wide receivers ever.

Gimmick Play — End reverse

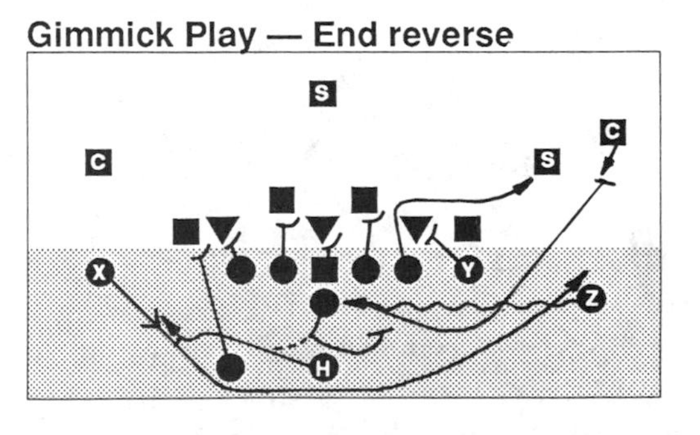

Gimmick Play — Fake Reverse

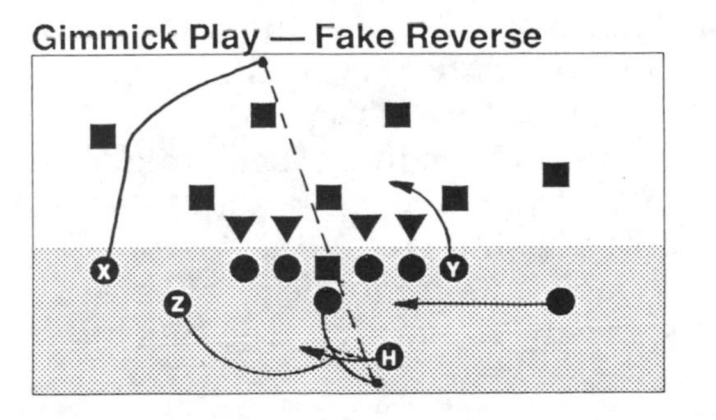

The Packers' James Lofton runs for a touchdown on an end reverse play.

End reverse. The strongside flanker runs in motion toward the ball and then back before taking on the left cornerback; the fullback blocks the weak outside linebacker; the strongside linemen slant downfield toward the weakside; the weakside guard blocks the weak inside backers; the quarterback reverses out and tosses the ball to the halfback. The receiver (X) pulls and heads toward the halfback, who hands him the ball. Running away from the flow of the play, the receiver reads the block on the cornerback before cutting upfield.

Fake reverse. This play can work if the flanker (Z) can throw the ball well. The quarterback takes a couple of steps back and pitches the ball to the running back swinging left; the running back turns to the flanker (Z) coming around and gives him the handoff on a reverse. The flanker fakes a run with a couple of steps, then drops back and throws downfield to the wide receiver (X), who has had a lot of time to put on a move to get past the cornerback.

CHAPTER FOUR

The Evolution of the Defense

In baseball, they say the game is 90 percent pitching. In golf, the saying is "Drive for show and putt for dough." And in football, the offense gets the most of the glamour and the glory.

But it's the defense that brings the championships. Look at the teams that win. They almost always have a rock-solid defense to go with a productive offense. It is unlikely you will see a high-scoring offense with a mediocre defense winning a Super Bowl. They might get close, but they won't get the trophy.

Defense is very simple: Stop the other team and get the ball back. "You should be looking for a turnover on every play," says Hall of Famer Alan Page.

Defensive coaches spend their time trying to anticipate what the offense is going to do, how to arrange the defense so it can't be blocked effectively, and how to load it one way or the other to stop the offense.

The defensive playbook is just as big as the offensive playbook. But playing defense is as much technique as tactics. Remember, defense is a reaction to the offense's action, so it is hard to diagram plays, although today's defenses often try to attack the offense before it is able to get going.

Defense needs coordination among individuals on the team. For example, there must be coordination between the middle linebacker and the two defensive tackles (or the inside linebackers and the nose tackle in the 3–4), just as there has to be coordination between the outside linebackers and the defensive ends; and the end, outside linebacker, and cornerback on either side must work as one unit. Vince Lombardi once said that defensive football consists of small teams working together within the whole team.

The biggest change for defenses in today's game is that they "attack" so much. The trend was really started by the Chicago Bears during their Super Bowl season of 1985. The Bears put relentless pressure on opposing quarterbacks and ballcarriers. Although this strategy left the Bears vulnerable to the long pass, they usually had the quarterback on the ground before he had a chance to find an open receiver. A strong pass rush makes for a daring, bold secondary that is not terrified of the deep pass. Defensive backs can then go for a big play.

There is also what's called the "bend-but-don't-break" defense. That's the one that doesn't mind giving up a lot of yards but doesn't want to give up a lot of points. A team with a weak pass rush might play the bend-but-don't-break style by playing "off" the receivers, letting them get open 10 to 15 yards downfield, but denying them the deeper routes. The hope of the defense is to get the ball on an interception or fumble.

A defensive call has only two or three elements: the front, which indicates the alignment and everyone's responsibility against the run; the pass coverage; and the blitz, if there is one.

After the snap of the ball, each defensive player reacts to a particular offensive player, his key. A linebacker's key would usually be the fullback. Because the fullback is a likely blocker for the halfback, and because offenses run to the strongside more often than not, simple logic tells you that keying the fullback in that situation

will probably lead the linebacker to the ball.

Defensive linemen key the man across from them. On any given play, the offensive linemen will do one of the following: drive toward the defensive lineman, pull left, pull right, back up in pass protection, or try to slip inside the defensive linemen. Whatever the offensive linemen do tells the defensive linemen the type of play being run and where the offensive players will go. In the secondary, the defensive backs consider down-and-distance, the offense's preferred formations, the score, and the field position. With that kind of knowledge, the defense has a good idea of what to expect.

Here's what the defensive captain might be thinking before the play begins: "It's third-and-four, they're in a slot formation, and 75 percent of the time they're in a slot, they run to the strongside. So we're going to overshift and try to meet them head on."

The defense that is called is really a front—the arrangement of the linemen and linebackers. The coverage is the style of pass defense to be played by the linebackers and deep backs.

On pass plays, defensive linemen want to avoid blockers so they can rush the passer. On running plays, a defensive lineman might take himself out of position if he sees the chance to make a tackle or funnel the ballcarrier toward a teammate. Defenses are also set up differently on runs than on passes. Defensive linemen might make their initial charge at an angle that makes them difficult to pass-block but easy to block for a run. So sometimes doing the right thing to stop a pass might be the wrong thing to stop a run.

In the early days of football, teams used a nine-man line. Then came lines with eight, seven, six, and five players. The four-man line dominated the 1960s and is still used today. The three-man line has been the most common front since the 1980s.

5–3 DEFENSE

Reducing the number of players on the defensive line to five, which put more players back into pass protection, was a bold move. It was probably first used in the NFL by the New York Giants in 1934 and became the standard pro defense for a decade.

5-3 Defense

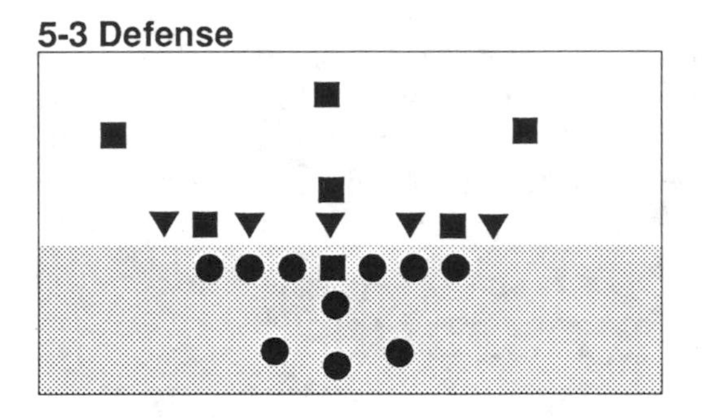

OKLAHOMA DEFENSE

Begun at the University of Oklahoma by the legendary coach Bud Wilkinson about 1947, the Oklahoma defense soon became the dominant defense in college football and strongly influenced pro defenses, but was mostly scoffed at until the Miami Dolphins adopted it in 1972, went undefeated, and won the Super Bowl. Look closely, and you will see the Oklahoma defense looks much like today's 3–4 defense.

Oklahoma Defense

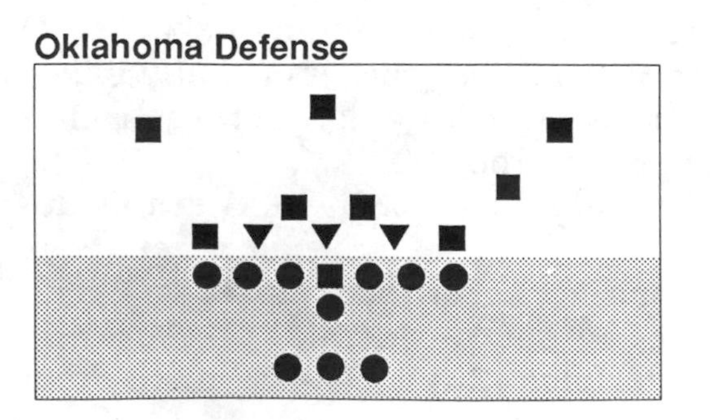

EAGLE DEFENSE

Eagle Defense

The Eagle defense was devised by Philadelphia Eagles coach Earle "Greasy" Neale in the 1940s to stop the T-formation. He set the defense in a 5–2–4, putting the linebackers a step or two off the line of scrimmage. The outside linebackers didn't have to cover deep passes, but did delay receivers and cover short passes. This was the first four-player secondary, but there was no middle linebacker. Although the Eagles won NFL championships in 1948 and '49, the defense was woefully weak over the middle. In 1950, Cleveland Browns coach Paul Brown beat the Eagles by splitting his ends wide and either throwing sideline passes to them or running his big fullback, Marion Motley, up the middle on a draw play, an innovation at the time.

UMBRELLA DEFENSE

In football, coaches are always scheming to stop the latest innovation. To stop fast receivers coming out of the backfield, New York Giants coach Steve Owen and his defensive captain, Tom Landry, devised the umbrella defense in 1950. The defensive backs were arranged in an umbrella-like shape with the defensive ends either rushing or dropping off the line to cover passes like later outside linebackers.

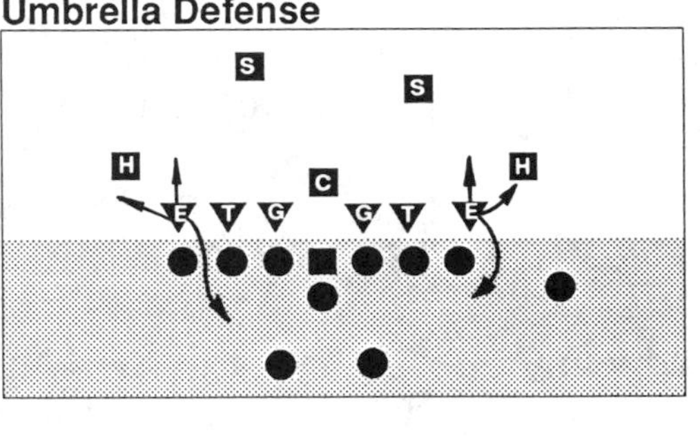
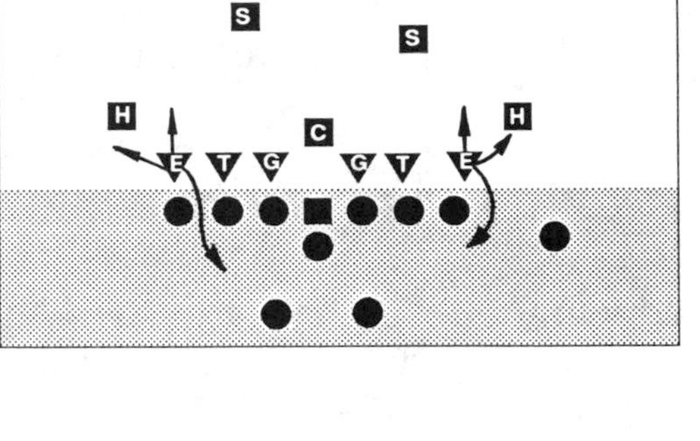
Umbrella Defense

4–3 DEFENSE

The outside linebackers grew out of the umbrella defense, and eventually the middle guard dropped off the line of scrimmage to become a middle linebacker. One of the outside linebackers usually plays on the line of scrimmage across from the tight end in the 4–3.

The advantage of the 4–3 is that it's a balanced defense that can meet most of the challenges of the offense, and the defense can put considerable pressure on the quarterback. But the 4–3 is more predictable than the 3–4.

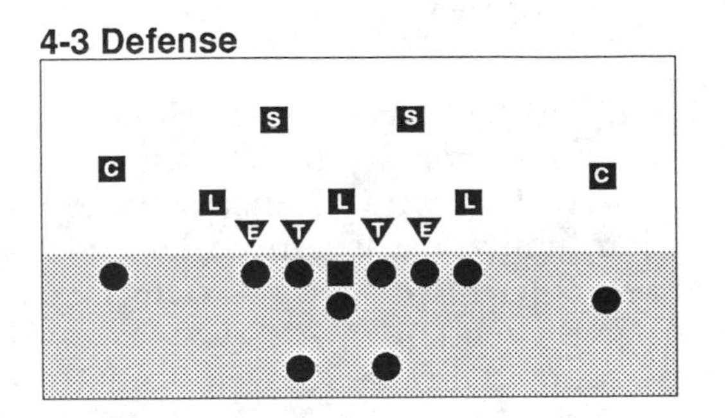
4-3 Defense

3–4 DEFENSE

The 3–4 defense is the most important defensive change in the past two decades. But it can be traced back to the University of Oklahoma in 1947, and it is also an offspring of the 5–2 Eagle defense of the '40s and '50s. The difference between the 3–4 and the 5–2 is that in the 3–4 the ends have become standup linebackers so they can cover passes. The 3–4 defense is now used by all but about a half dozen teams. In the 3–4, three linemen rush the passer, and a linebacker is kept in reserve as a potential designated blitzer, like Lawrence Taylor of the New York Giants. The trick with this outside linebacker is to keep the offense guessing—will he rush, or will he drop into coverage? On running plays, the defensive linemen try to tie up as many offensive linemen as they can so the linebackers can make the tackles.

3-4 Defense

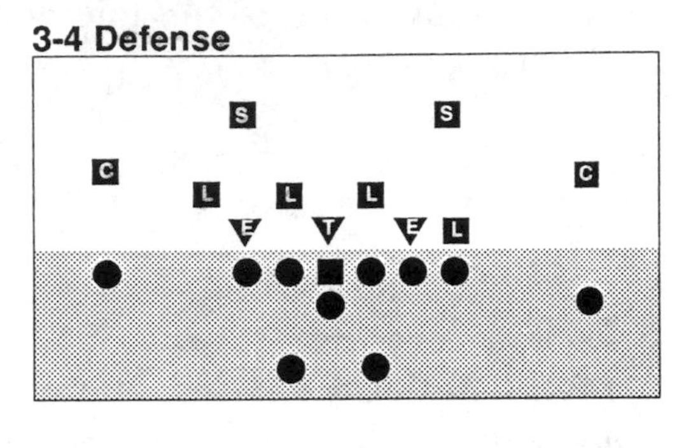

The fourth linebacker provides more flexibility near the line of scrimmage than a fourth lineman in that the 3–4 allows greater potential for stopping the run and gives better pass coverage. Defenses can stunt—that is, switch assignments to create new attack lanes after the offense has lined up. Any one of four linebackers can blitz. The 3–4 gives the linebackers better angles to blitz from. But, on the negative side, the 3–4 mounts less consistent pressure on the quarterback.

VARIATIONS OF THE 4–3 DEFENSE

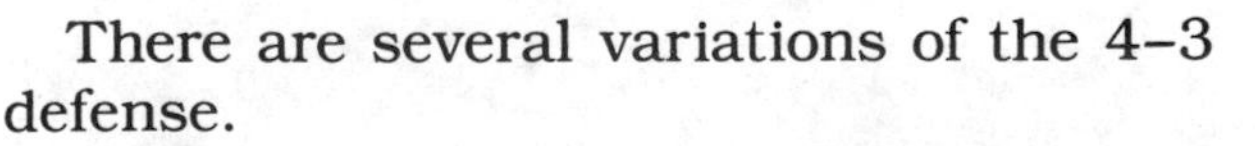

There are several variations of the 4–3 defense.

Stunt 4–3. Pittsburgh would put tackle Joe Greene at a 45-degree angle in the gap between a guard and center, and put middle linebacker Jack Lambert behind Greene. This helped the Pittsburgh Steelers win four Super Bowls in the

Stunt 4-3

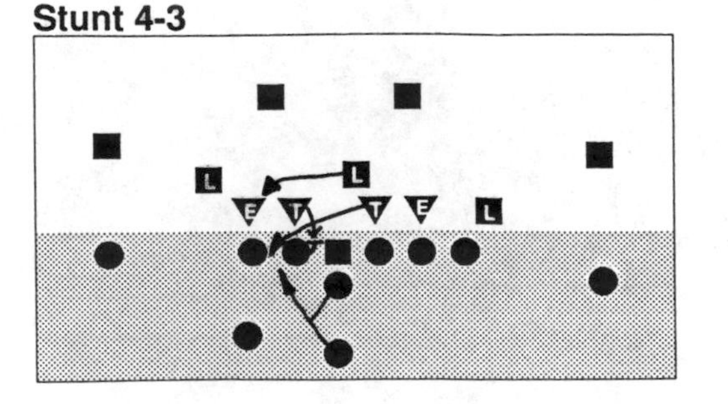

1980s. Of course, it also helps if both players are future Hall of Famers.

Over and Under Defenses. Defenses often try to put more defensive linemen near the expected point of attack. So, in an over defense, all four members of the defensive front shift one position over toward the strongside of the offensive formation. An under shift is exactly the opposite, because the defensive line shifts away from the strongside. There are other variations in which only some of the linemen shift positions.

4-3 Under

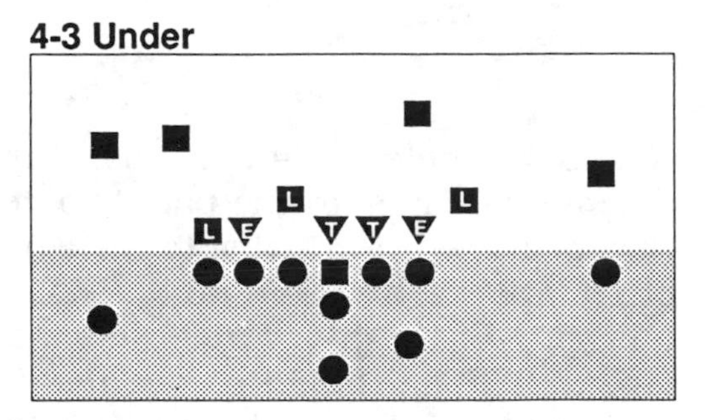

4-3 Over

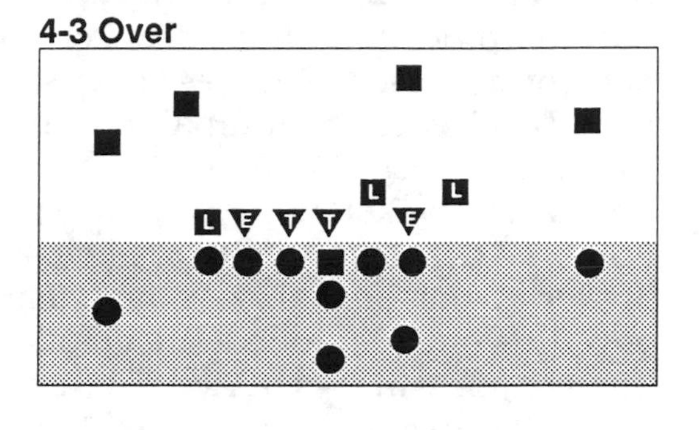

Flex. The flex defense was pioneered by Tom Landry's Dallas Cowboys, and was rarely used by any other team. The flex set two linemen (on a 4–3 line) off the line of scrimmage two or three yards, and was geared toward stopping runs. The two offset linemen would read the combinations of blocks they saw, while the other linemen attacked and clogged up the blocking patterns. Although the Cowboys continued to use it through 1988, it didn't work as well in recent years because pro football turned into a passing game. The diagram above shows how the flex defense worked against a sweep run from an I-Formation.

Flex Defense

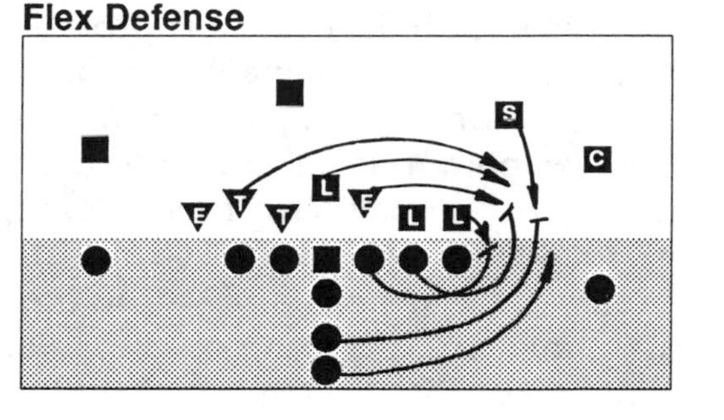

CHAPTER FIVE

Defensive Tactics

As already mentioned, today's defenses have started to attack, trying to force offenses to react before they have a chance to act. Defenses can do a lot of things to force the action.

THE BLITZ

Every team blitzes these days. They have to. They can't just sit back and let the offenses dictate the rhythm. Many teams blitz the most when they're backed up inside their own 20-yard line in an attempt to push the opponent back to the 30 and thus out of easy field-goal range.

The blitz was first seen in the 1950s. Teams were passing so much at that time that the defense had to come up with an innovation to rush the passer. Thus, the blitz (originally called red dog) was born.

In a blitz, everybody usually covers man-to-man, although double-coverage is possible, except for the player or players blitzing. The main idea of the blitz is either to spring a defender free or to get one-on-one blocking for all the pass rushers. For the blitz to succeed, it is not necessary that a blitzer actually be the one to reach the quarterback. The strategy is just as effective if a defensive tackle gets the quarterback because the blocker who would have double-teamed him had to block the blitzer instead.

Some linebackers are blessed with breathtaking speed and are able to take control of a play before it gets started. More than anything, blitzing breaks up the timing of the offense and confuses its blocking. It's one of the most dramatic plays in the game and can be effective against both the run and the pass. Defenses use a blitz to confuse opponents, just as offenses use men in motion before the snap. Either way, the opponent doesn't know where the danger will come from.

Even the threat of a blitz—a fake blitz—can be as effective as the real thing. A defense can act as if it is going to blitz, then drop back at the hike of the ball. There's also the *fake* fake blitz.

The safety blitz—in which a defender streaks from deep in the secondary toward

The New York Giants' linebacker Lawrence Taylor blitzes.

the quarterback—is one version of the blitz. This tactic can be traced to Larry Wilson, the Hall of Fame free safety for the St. Louis Cardinals in the 1960s. The safety blitz can dump the passer for a big loss and give the defense a boost. Or it can end in disaster. In Super Bowl X, the Dallas Cowboys' Cliff Harris blitzed Pittsburgh's Terry Bradshaw, but the Steeler quarterback got off a game-winning 64-yard bomb to Lynn Swann in an area Harris could have helped cover.

There are two ways for offenses to beat a blitz: block all the blitzers or throw the ball before they reach the quarterback. Teams usually try to do the latter.

Lawrence Taylor Blitz

Lawrence Taylor of the New York Giants may be the most feared defensive player in the NFL today. Disaster often occurs when a team assigns its remaining back to block Taylor, because he thrives on getting to the quarterback from his weak outside linebacker position. To cover for Taylor, the Giants' weak inside linebacker covers a back out of the backfield. Getting to the quarterback on this play means Taylor (56) has to get by only the fullback.

Lawrence Taylor Blitz

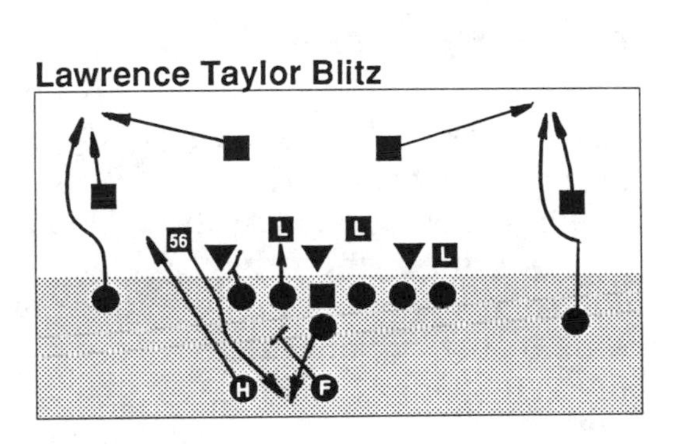

Middle Linebacker Blitz

A blitz by the middle linebacker is usually in coordination with one of the defensive tackles. For example, the middle linebacker can blitz to the strongside, with the strongside defensive tackle taking the inside, or he can blitz to the weakside with the weakside defensive tackle taking the inside. Or he could blitz right up the middle with both defensive tackles taking the outside.

Middle Linebacker Blitz

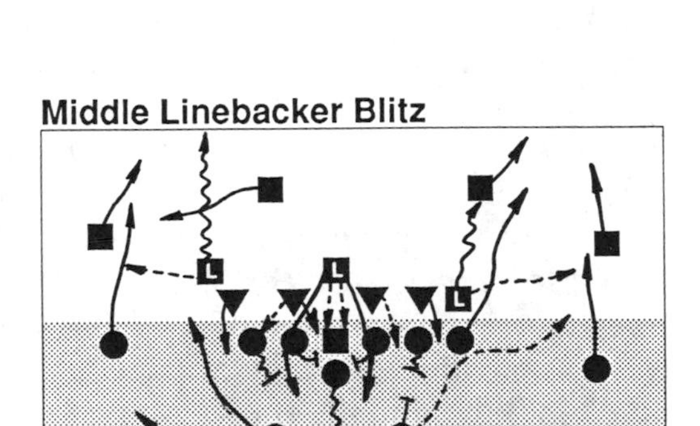

Safety Blitz

The weak (free) safety blitzes more often than the strong safety. As the diagram shows, even if the offense keeps a back in to pick up the rush, the pressure is severe because a blitz by the safety is usually not anticipated.

Safety Blitz

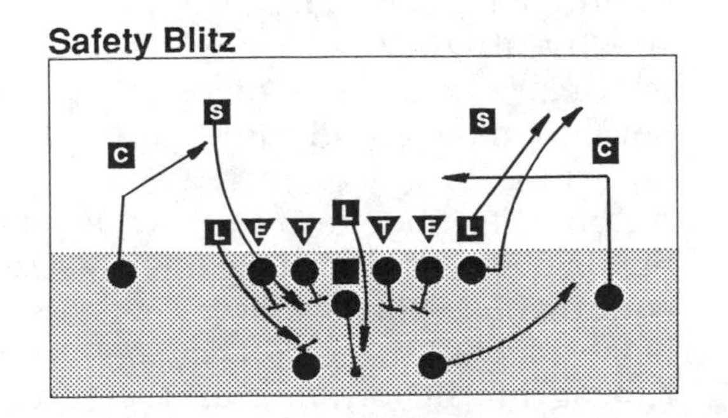

DEFENSIVE GAMES

Stunts, stacks, and slants are effective tactics in which defensive linemen use unexpected moves to get past blockers to the runner or quarterback. During a game, you will see defensive linemen constantly moving around, setting up in different positions. They're trying to expose and take advantage of weaknesses found in the offense.

Stunts. Stunts change the responsibility of two or more players, while everyone else continues his own basic responsibilities. Stunts confuse blocking assignments, exert pressure at the point of attack, and break up the offense's timing.

The simplest stunt is a change stunt, in which a defensive tackle and a linebacker change positions. The hope is that a blocker will lose track of one of them, or that blockers will run into each other trying to follow them, like a pick in basketball. There are end-tackle stunts, in which the end pinches in and tries to contain two men and the tackle loops around him; tackle-end stunts, which are the reverse; tackle-tackle stunts; and deep loops, in which a player might swoop in from two positions away. There are also all kinds of stunts with the linebackers.

The Minnesota Vikings' defensive coordinator, Floyd Peters, says, "The obvious key to stunting is the ability of one man to tie up two. You've got three and a half seconds, tops, so you have to work your games to get something open quickly."

Offenses have solved the problem of stunting somewhat by zone blocking—blocking whoever comes into a player's area.

Stunts

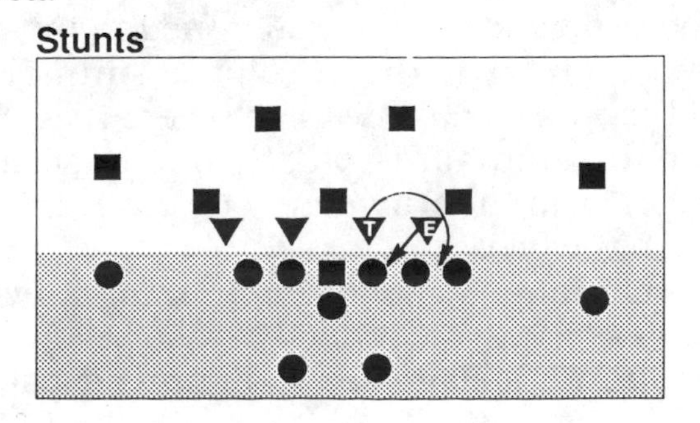

Stacks. Stacking is lining up one or more of the linebackers directly behind the linemen, a little like hiding them, to keep offensive linemen away from them. In this way, the Kansas City Chiefs beat the Minnesota Vikings in Super Bowl IV, and the Baltimore Colts beat the Dallas Cowboys the next year. "The advantage of the stack is that the offense doesn't know whether the linebacker will peel off to the right or left, or barge in straight ahead," said former Chiefs head coach Hank Stram.

Stacking

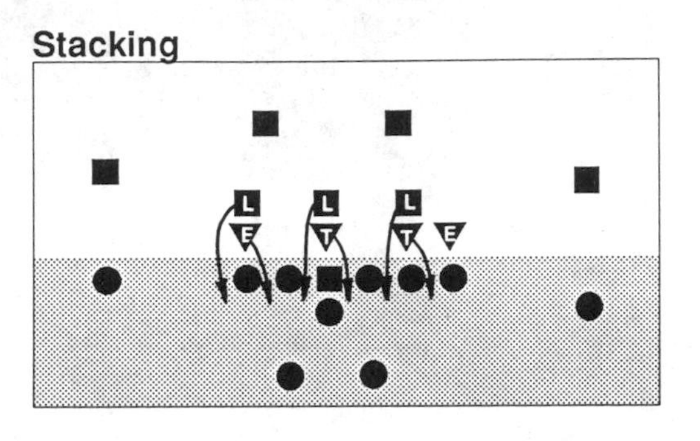

Slants. A slant is a charge by a defensive lineman to the left or right instead of straight ahead.

Slants

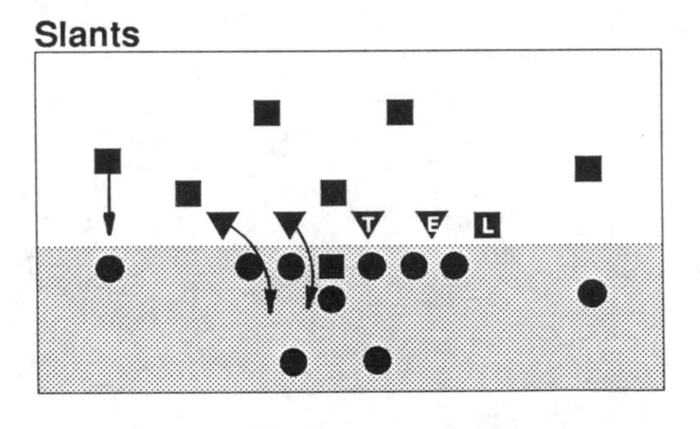

Force. A defense must protect certain areas of the field. One of these is the outside on a running play. A cornerback or safety must not let a ballcarrier get outside him, because he might be the last defender between the runner and the goal line. The defender has to force the runner back toward the middle of the field and contain the play. Determining which defensive player is the force man depends on the split of the wide receiver. The strong safety usually calls out who will force and

who will stay back in pass coverage. Linebackers also occasionally force.

Cornerback Force. If the wide receiver is set in close—less than 10 yards off the line—the cornerback usually has force responsibilities.

Cornerback Force

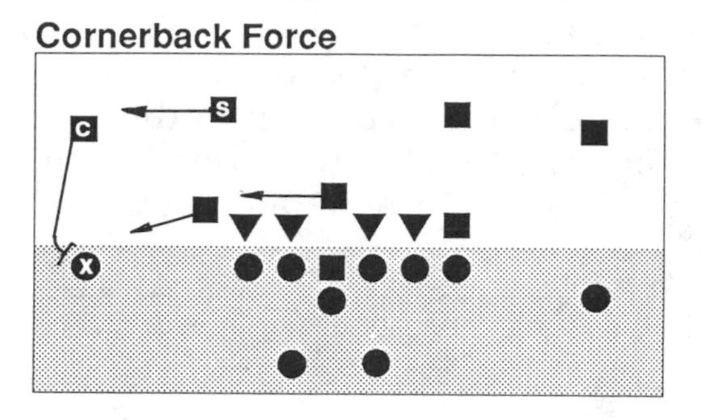

Safety Force. The safety becomes the force man when the wide receiver is split outside more than 10 yards.

Safety Force

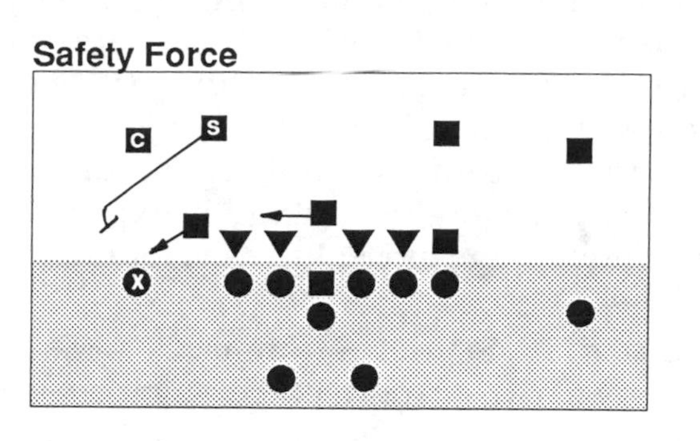

PASS DEFENSE

There are two main pass coverages: man-to-man and zone.

Man to Man Coverage

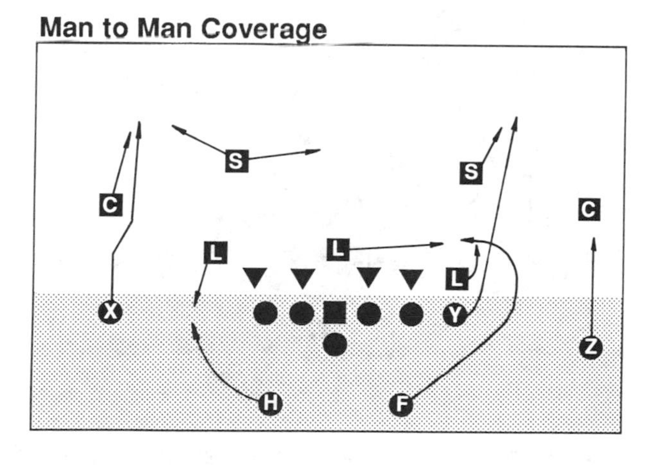

Zone Defense

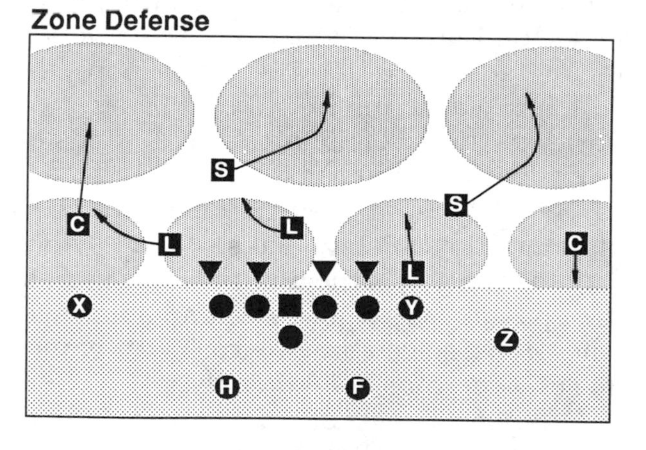

Man-to-Man Coverage. Man-to-man is the simplest defense. Linebackers and defensive backs play against the running back or receiver to whom they have been assigned. They hook up with the receiver as he leaves the line of scrimmage and stay with him until the play is over. In man-to-man, the defensive backs cover the ends, the tight end, and the halfback in single coverage. The free safety either helps out or covers the halfback, and the linebackers key the fullback. Man-to-man could be broken down into (1) bump-and-run, where defenders are positioned right off the receiver at the line of scrimmage; (2) the traditional coverage where they are four to seven yards off the line of scrimmage; or (3) intermediate coverage, in between the two.

Technique is everything in man-to-man defense. Pass defenders are particularly careful of their pre-snap alignment, back-

pedal, and position on the receiver. Most important is concentration, looking at the receiver's numbers, not his eyes, and certainly not at the quarterback, until the receiver makes his final move. When the ball is in the air, the defender is supposed to be in a position to break through the receiver or to step in front of him to take the ball at its highest point. If a defender can't get to the ball, he has to be in a position to grasp the receiver.

Man-to-man coverage puts a great deal of pressure on the cornerbacks and the strong safety. It is very difficult to control the post routes (bombs down the middle) because there is little help on the inside. More and more, teams are using zone defenses.

3-4 Zone

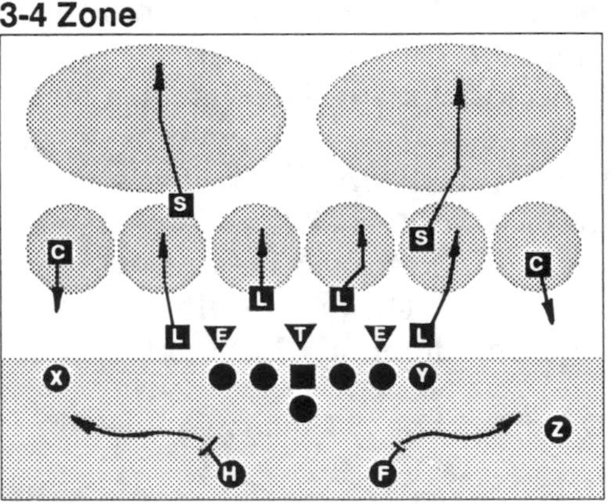

Combination Zone

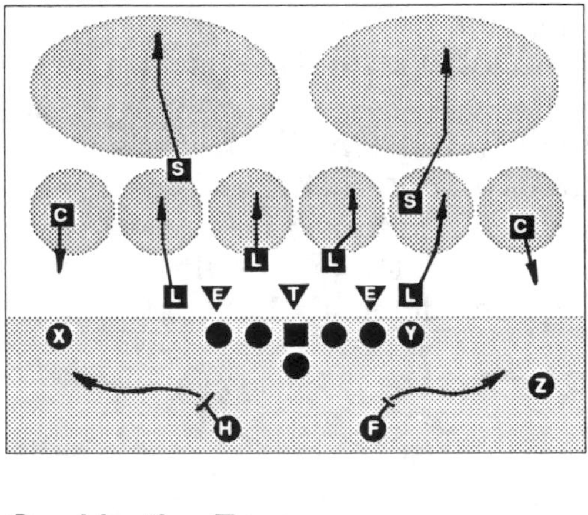

Zone Coverage. Zone defenses started to be used a lot in the late 1960s, although they date back to the '40s and '50s. Zone defense is simply covering an area of the field, rather than a specific receiver, and it works best in stopping the long passes. Zone defense reverses the saying that "offense acts and defense reacts." Zone defenders do not follow the receiver's initiative, as in man-to-man coverage. Because they cover certain parts of the field, they can dictate where the offense runs its routes.

The basic theory is to get every area, or zone, covered, and to create movement so that the quarterback and receivers are working against a constantly shifting scene. There are seven zones in a 4–3 defense and eight zones in the 3–4. Zone defenses are further broken down into strong and weakside rotations, double zones, and half zones.

Here's how a zone works: At the snap, the strongside cornerback "rolls up"—meaning he steps forward into the teeth of the strongside, where the fullback, the flanker, and the tight end might be running their patterns. As the strongside cornerback is rotating up, everybody else is "taking drops," moving back to the deepest and widest boundaries of their zones. They then wait for the play to unfold. As the receivers begin to enter the zones, the defenders start to move together, tightening the amount of open territory.

The main weakness of zone defenses is that a short passing game can pick them apart because the quarterback is throwing underneath the linebackers (especially over the middle) and to the sides (the "seams"). (Zone defenses also leave gaping holes for running plays.) There are open seams between the zones, and a good passer can hit a receiver in these cracks. That's why teams that play zone tend to have a strong pass rush that denies the passer time to "read" the coverage and figure out where the openings are. Zone defenses can be stretched horizontally (deep) with a fast receiver, or vertically with patterns to the sidelines or in the flats to running backs (which is one reason why running backs catch so many passes today). The offense can also "flood" a zone with two receivers.

There are many combinations of zone defenses, and no quarterback is given the luxury of seeing the same "look" in the defense two plays in a row. Combination defenses are a combination of zone, man-to-man, and double-teaming. The defense could be a half zone, in which one side of the secondary plays man while the other side plays zone, or a combination of man coverage shallow and zone coverage deep. Or it could be a key, in which some defenders, by reading predesigned keys, will switch from zone to man, or vice versa.

The weakness of a combination defense's double coverage of a dangerous receiver is that in order to cover one man with two men, the team is leaving itself open for flares by the fullback and screens to the halfback, and for post patterns by the wide receiver on the strong side.

There are dozens of different types of zone coverages. In fact, the Chicago Bears and Philadelphia Eagles might have 60 different zone coverages, whereas the Los Angeles Raiders have played mainly man-to-man for years.

Multiple Defensive Backs. A fifth defensive back is usually used in situations where the offense is likely to pass. The fifth defensive back, called the nickel back ("N" in the diagram) can be placed anywhere in the secondary. He usually covers the third wide receiver, most often the slot man, man-to-man with deep help from a safety. At other times, the nickel back will drop back and play "centerfield," like a free safety.

The dime defensive back ("D" in the diagrams) a sixth defensive back replacing another linebacker, is used when the defense is certain the offense will pass.

A seventh defensive back, usually called the quarter or seven penny ("Q" in the diagram for Quarter Defense) is used quite often these days. The biggest weakness of having seven defensive backs is that such a defensive alignment is very easy to run against. A few teams have used as many as two down linemen and nine backs (linebackers and defensive backs).

Nickel Defense (5 Defensive Backs)

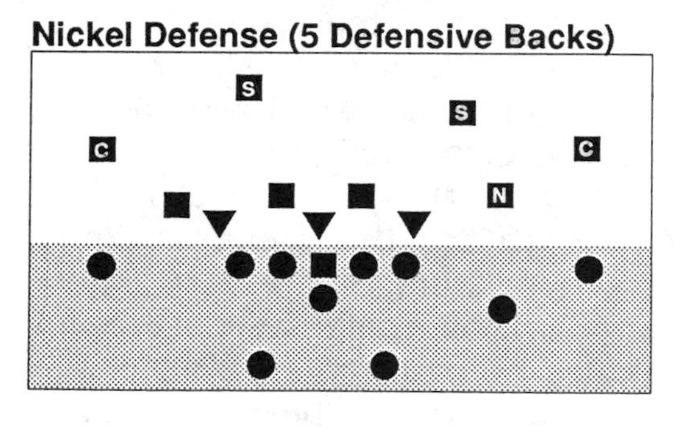

Dime Defense (6 Defensive Backs)

Quarter Defense (7 Defensive Backs)

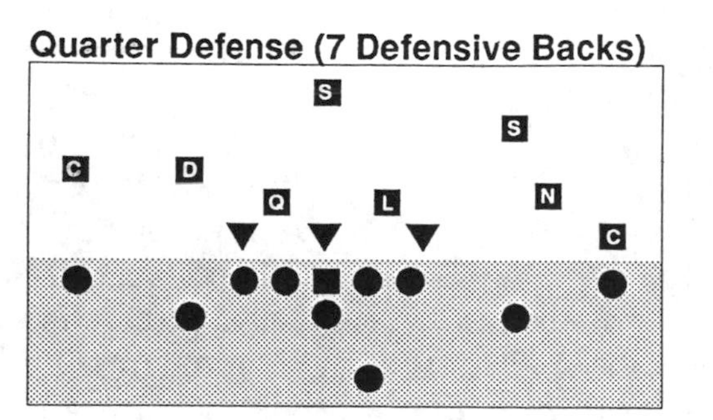

SPECIAL DEFENSES

Run Defense. The diagram shows a good run defense from a 3–4. It features penetration by the blitzing weak outside linebacker and coordinated moves by the weak inside backer and the defensive end. If the offense calls a passing play, the defensive backs simply stay back instead of moving foward.

Run Defense

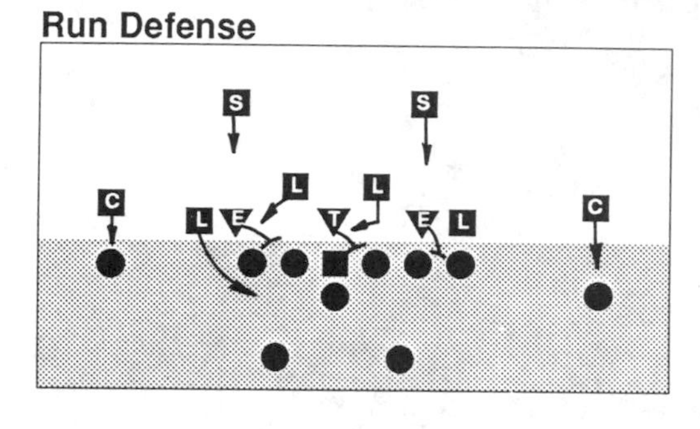

Goal-line Defense. When the offense is inside its opponent's 10-yard line, about to score a touchdown, goal-line defenses bring in extra linemen. These substitutes set up in the gaps between each offensive player to fill every hole in the line. Sometimes two or three deep players will stay off the line to stop surprise passes.

Goal-line Defense

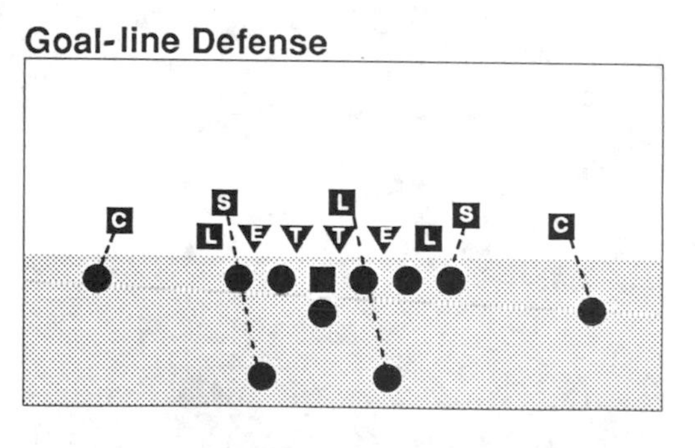

The New Orleans Saints' goal-line defense tries to stop the Bears' Walter Payton.

Prevent Defense. A prevent defense involves trying to prevent the offense from completing passes and winning a game in the last two minutes. The defense rushes only three people and drops off eight players into pass coverage. The theory behind the prevent defense is to allow short passes and to tackle receivers before they get out of bounds. This keeps the clock running. Usually, however, prevent defenses prevent little because, given the luxury of time, most quarterbacks can complete a pass against only three pass rushers.

CHAPTER SIX

The Special Teams

Special teams are the "third team"—besides the offense and defense—of football. Their success or failure in advancing the ball can put one of the other two units in position to win a game, or lose one. Special teams get the least attention from coaches and fans, but they are one of the most important parts of football, part of both the offense and defense.

Until 20 years ago, no team had a special-teams coach. Now every team has one. Here's why: One out of every seven plays involves the special teams, and 33 percent of all points are scored by special teams. Special teams are involved in plays with more total yard gain per game than the yards compiled by both offenses. It took a long time, but the NFL is finally putting a lot of emphasis on special teams.

Kicking is the biggest part of special teams. At least one of three things characterizes all kicks: a large amount of yardage, usually 40 yards or more; a change of ball possession; or a specific attempt to score points.

Return teams can get that long run for a touchdown or set up a touchdown to turn the game around. Coverage teams can stop the opponent deep in its own territory and set up the defense in good field position. The special teams' real job, then, is support, because they appear in between the time the offense has the ball and the defense is trying to get it.

Special team players are called the suicide squads and the kamikaze squads. But they work from diagrams in a playbook just as the offensive and defensive players do.

The biggest fear of special teams is to have a kick returned all the way for a touchdown. Although fewer than 10 punts and kickoffs are returned for a touchdown in an average season, it's the most demoralizing play in football.

KICKOFFS

Kickoffs

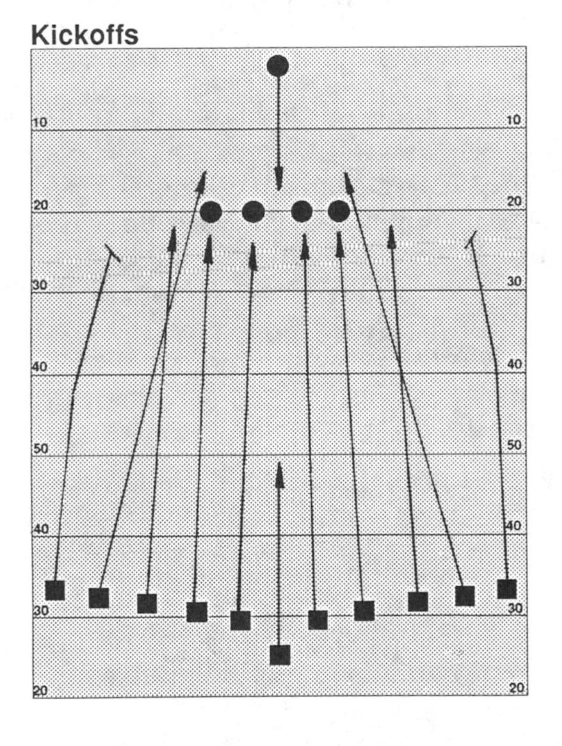

Members of the team have one responsibility on kickoffs: contain the ball and the man carrying it. Everyone is assigned a lane of coverage. The players race downfield abreast, careful to keep their own lane of attack; otherwise a weak spot can be created. Along the two outside lanes are the two force men whose job is to turn the ballcarrier back in to the center of the field, where he can be tackled by the other players. Coaches demand gang tackling to

increase the chances of a fumble and recovery close to the goal line.

Occasionally you will see an onside kick when a team is losing late in the game and needs the ball back. The idea is to kick the ball to make it bounce high, like a jump ball in basketball. The kick must travel at least 10 yards. The kicking team knows where the ball is supposed to go, so that gives it about a 50–50 chance to recover it. The team expecting an onside kick usually puts in players used to handling the ball, like running backs and receivers. Once the ball goes 10 yards, it's up for grabs.

KICKOFF RETURN

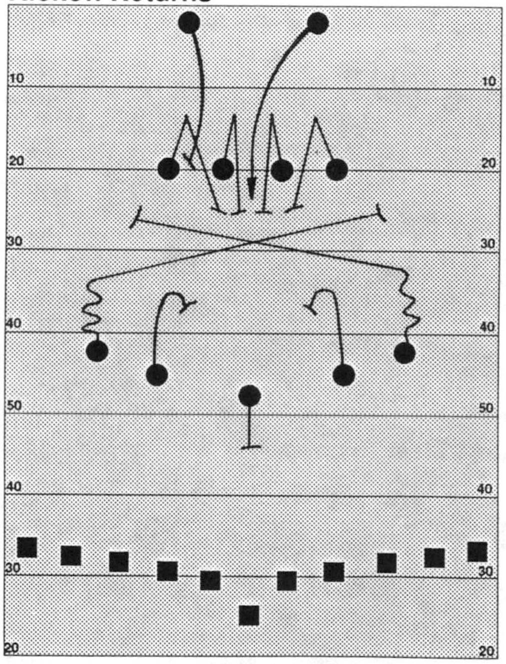

There are three separate groups of players on a kickoff return team. The first wave is five blockers, the second is the four-man wedge, and the third is the two returners.

There are also three types of kickoff returns: middle, left, and right. At the time of the kickoff, the wedge of blockers begin their retreat, falling back for the returner to run behind, and they must be ready to meet the onslaught of rushing tacklers in an effort to pry open a little daylight for the returner. The returner follows the wedge until he sees an opening, and from there he's on his own. The goal of a kickoff return is to set up the offense at its own 30-yard line.

Kickoff Returns

PUNTING

Punting teams want to drive their opponents in the other direction as far as possible. Ideally, the snap should take eight-tenths of a second and the punter should get the ball off in another 1.3 seconds. Any longer than 2.1 seconds risks a blocked punt. Then, you want your punter to have at least four seconds of hangtime (the

Punt Coverage

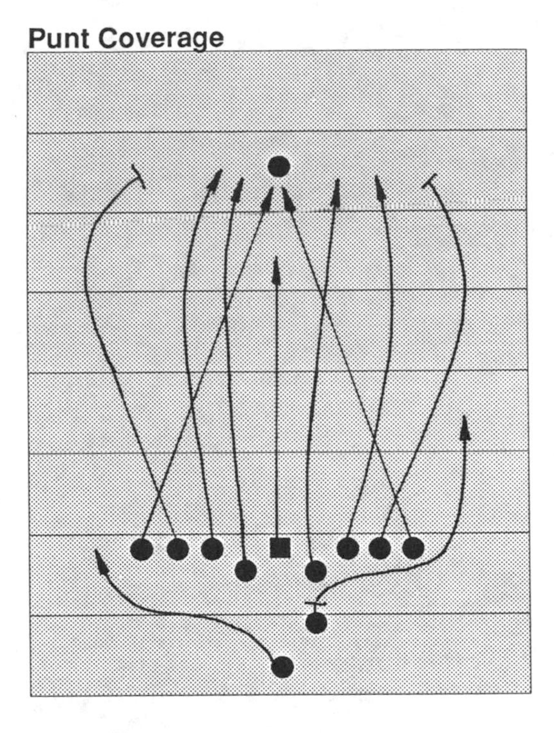

Punt Return

length of time a punt is in the air). Punters don't want to outkick their coverage, so a punter who gets a lot of hangtime is valuable. He never wants to kick the ball into the end zone. If he does, his team will lose 20 yards—the kick's distance. The goal of the punt-coverage team is to stop the return man as quickly as possible after he has caught the ball.

As one special-teams coach says: "If your man hits one for 60 yards, but it stays up only four seconds and is returned for 30 yards, you net only 30 yards, not good enough. We'd rather have shorter, higher kicks hanging so long that the return man is surrounded when he catches the ball."

PUNT RETURN

Punt returns are supposed to go to either the left or the right. Punt returners are seldom able to run up the middle because the hangtime allows the kicking team to get downfield. Blockers then set up a wall to either side of the field for the runner to run behind.

If the return team wants to try to block the punt, they usually mass a large number of players against one part of the offensive line in an all-out effort to get to the punter. Punt blockers are instructed to

The Saints' Morten Anderson kicks a field goal.

aim for a point two yards in front of the expected impact of the punter's foot and the football, so they don't rough the punter and get penalized.

FIELD-GOAL AND EXTRA-POINT ATTEMPT

Both field goals and extra points are kicked in the same basic manner. The holder and kicker work together to make sure they get the kick off in 1.3 seconds. Taking any longer risks a blocked kick. As shown in the diagrams, the holder sets up for placement of the ball seven yards behind the center. A fake field goal is one of football's most exciting plays—and one of its most risky, because it gambles a reasonably sure three points for a chance to score a touchdown.

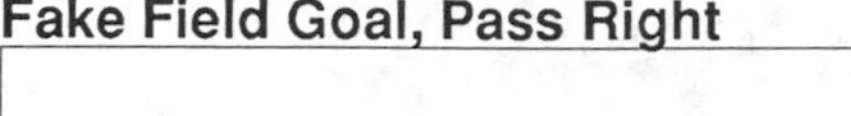
Field Goal, Extra-Point Attempt

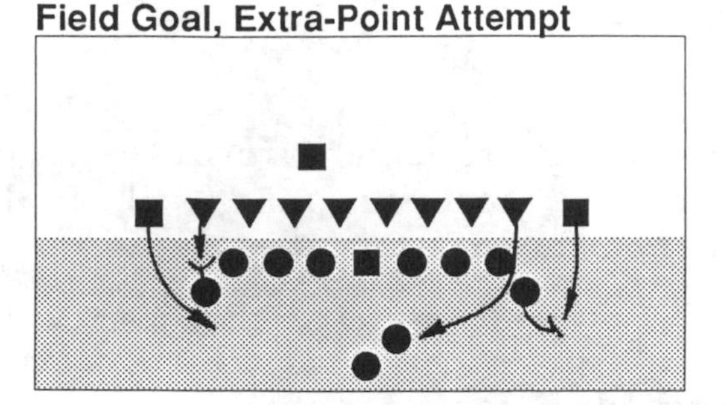

Fake Field Goal, Pass Right

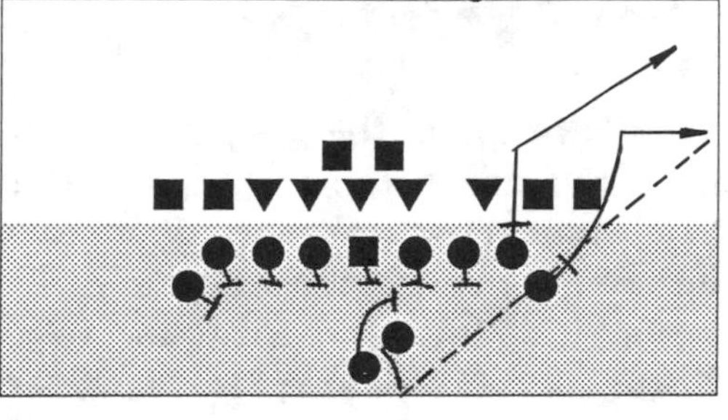

BLOCKING KICKS

Blocking a field goal can really turn a game around. The block negates a possible three-point advantage and gives the opposing team the ball. Tall linemen fill the middle and either try to break through the offensive line to block the kick or leap high in the air to bat down a kick. The players on the outside have a direct angle to block the kick—if they get therc in time.

Blocking a Field Goal

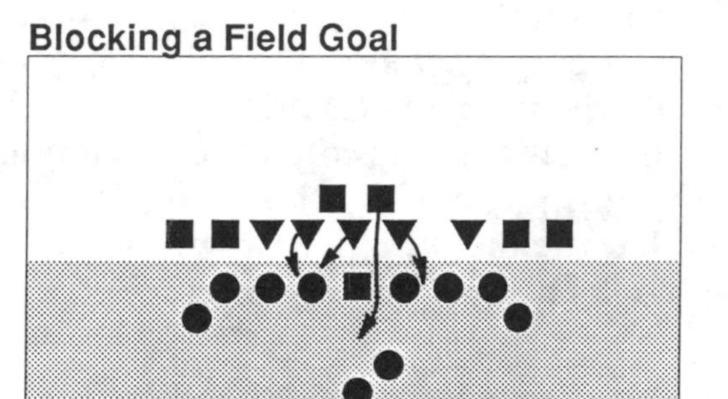

CHAPTER SEVEN

Great Plays by Great Players

Following are some favorite plays by some of the greatest running backs in the history of the NFL.

JIM BROWN QUICK TOSS

The quick toss is the fastest way to get outside and turn the corner. It was a favorite of the man most pro football historians consider the greatest player ever—Jim Brown of the Cleveland Browns. To compound the element of surprise, it was usually run from a quick count.

To make this play work, the tight end, lined up left, blocked the right linebacker; the strongside tackle pulled and led interference with the strongside guard blocking the defensive right end; the center blocked the middle linebacker; and the weak tackle slid through the line to pick up defenders trying to move across the field. The halfback led the blocking for Brown, who read the blocks before turning the corner.

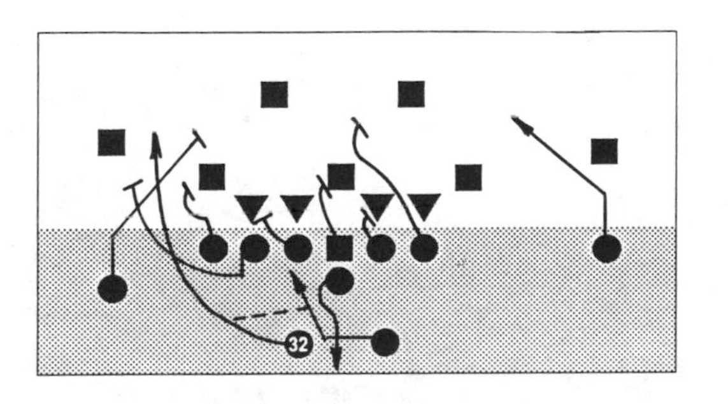

GALE SAYERS SWEEP

A formation and play tailored to the explosive running ability of Gale Sayers, the Chicago Bears' Hall of Fame running back in the 1960s, worked like this: The Bears lined up in a triple wing, usually a passing formation. The idea was to spread out the defense, because once Sayers got into open field, it was almost impossible for one player to tackle him. The left guard pulled to lead interference and blocked the right cornerback; the left flanker took out the strong safety; and the slotback blocked the defensive right end. Notice that no one was assigned to block the defensive left end. Sayers would take a lateral from the quarterback and run toward the sideline, cutting upfield depending on the blocks.

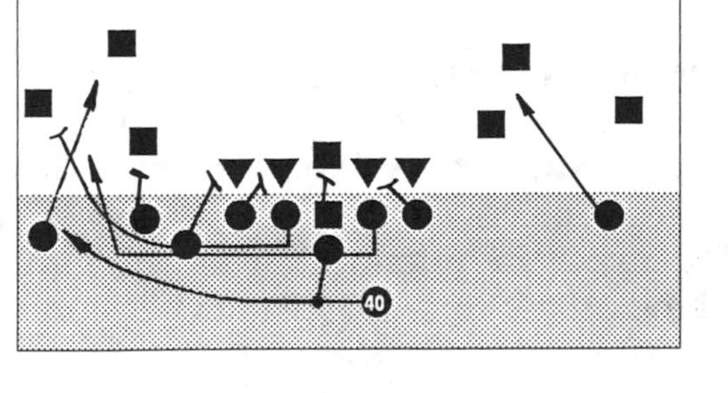

O. J. SIMPSON SWEEP

Many of the Buffalo Bills' plays in the 1970s were designed to break loose O. J. Simpson, in an attempt to get him into the open where he could "freelance."

In this play, the strongside guard pulls and blocks the right linebacker; the tight end and strongside tackle pinch in and take out the defensive right end and tackle; the right guard pulls and blocks the strongside cornerback; and the flanker blocks the strong safety. The quarterback fakes a handoff to the other running back, who hits the line off-tackle. Simpson would take the real handoff and turn left end, where there is usually good blocking support.

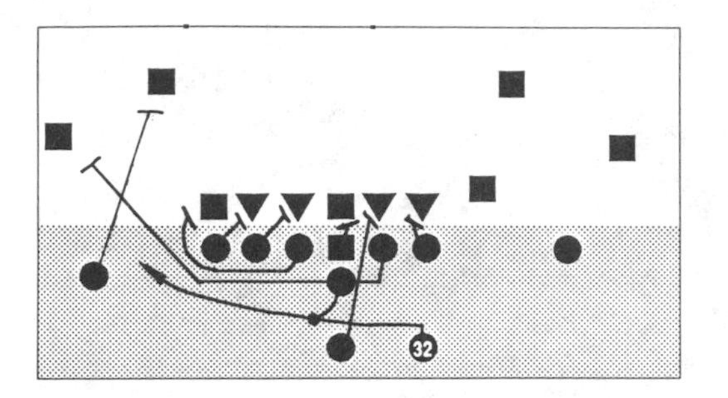

Buffalo Bills Hall of Famer O. J. Simpson runs the sweep.

FRANCO HARRIS FULLBACK TRAP

Franco Harris ran a fullback trap play several times during a game as the Pittsburgh Steelers won four Super Bowls in the 1970s.

To make this play work, halfback Rocky Bleier runs motion right and blocks the strongside cornerback; the tight end blocks the defensive end to the inside; the strongside tackle traps the strongside outside linebacker; the strongside guard hooks around to ward off the strongside inside linebacker; the weak guard and center double-team the nose tackle, then the center slips off the block and picks up the weakside linebacker. While all this is going on, Harris takes the handoff from quarterback Terry Bradshaw and reads the blocks by the tight end and the trapping tackle before making his cut either inside or outside.

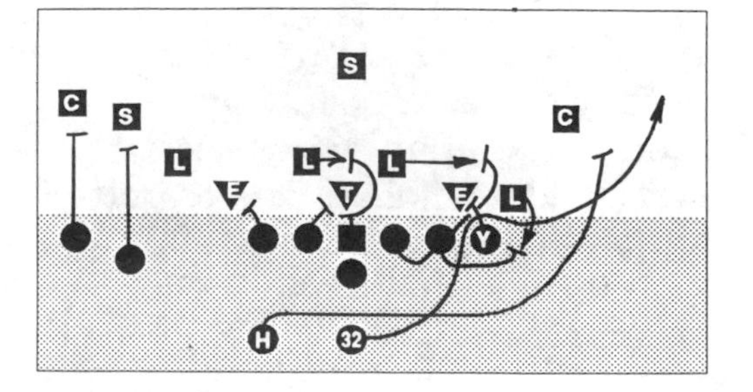

EARL CAMPBELL 34M

Earl Campbell of the Houston Oilers was one of the best running backs of the late 1970s, especially when running the 34M play from the I-formation. He had a unique ability to pick his way through the point of attack on the defense's strong side of a 4–3.

The key to the success of this play is the block of the strongside tackle on the defensive end. The strong guard and center double-team the defensive tackle; the weakside tackle makes contact with the end, then picks up the weak inside linebacker; the slotback slants inside to cut off the defensive end; and the tight end controls the strong outside linebacker. After taking the handoff from quarterback Dan Pastorini, Campbell reads the strongside tackle's block and the point of attack.

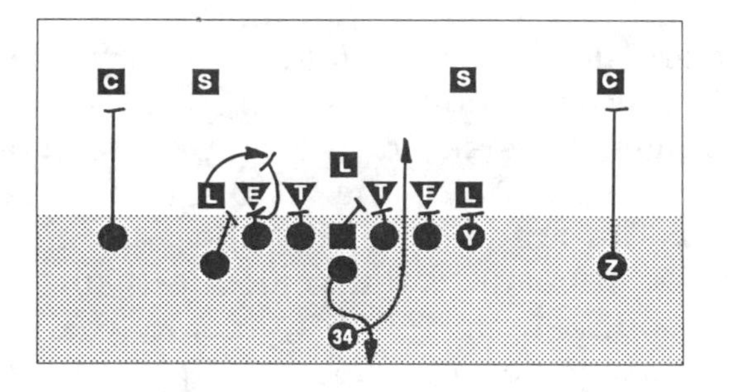

TONY DORSETT SWEEP

Tony Dorsett of the Dallas Cowboys was one of the quickest running backs in NFL history, and this play used his speed to the fullest. The sweep depended on Dorsett's ability to follow the strongside guard who was pulling to lead interference.

To make this play work, the tight end and strongside tackle double-team the defensive left end; the tight end slips off that block and picks up the middle linebacker; the strongside guard pulls to block the strong safety; the fullback hooks or kicks out the strong linebacker; the center reaches out to block the defensive left tackle; and the weakside offensive linemen block their opponents. Dorsett takes a pitch from quarterback Roger Staubach and cuts inside or outside of the force man (the strong safety).

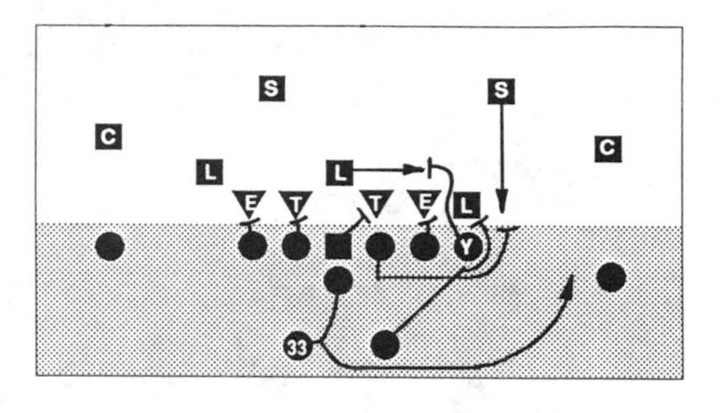

WALTER PAYTON TOSS 49 TWIST

Walter Payton of the Chicago Bears ran this favorite play six or seven times a game for years.

Here's what it involves: The tight end blocks the defensive end; the strongside tackle pulls and blocks the strong linebacker; the strongside guard pulls to lead interference downfield; the fullback (Payton's buddy Roland Harper) blocks the strong safety; the wide receivers influence the cornerbacks to backpedal before making their cuts; the center cuts off the lateral pursuit of the weak outside linebacker; and the weakside guard steps forward to block the nose tackle. Payton takes the pitch and cuts upfield. Occasionally, he passes to the flanker.

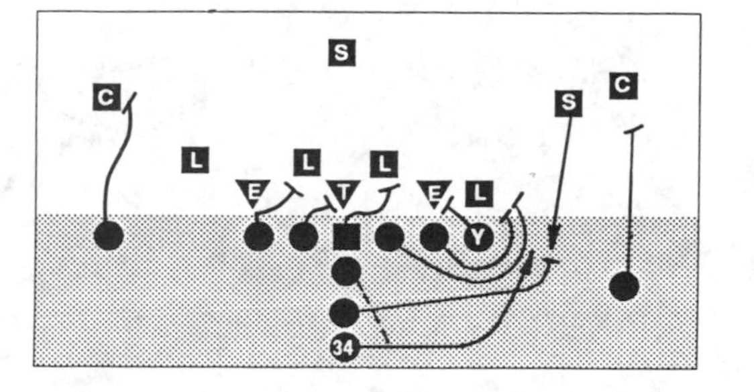

All-time rushing leader Walter Payton runs his favorite play.

JOHN RIGGINS 70-CHIP

On a fourth-and-one play in Super Bowl XVII, with everyone expecting a run up the middle, John Riggins, the Washington Redskins' bruising fullback, ran for a 43-yard touchdown.

Clint Didier, the third tight end in Washington's lineup, went into motion, then looped back toward his position. The object was to create confusion for the defense and make it difficult to set. Riggins took a pitch from Joe Theismann and followed the blocking of the halfback, leading him to a hole between the left tackle and the left end.

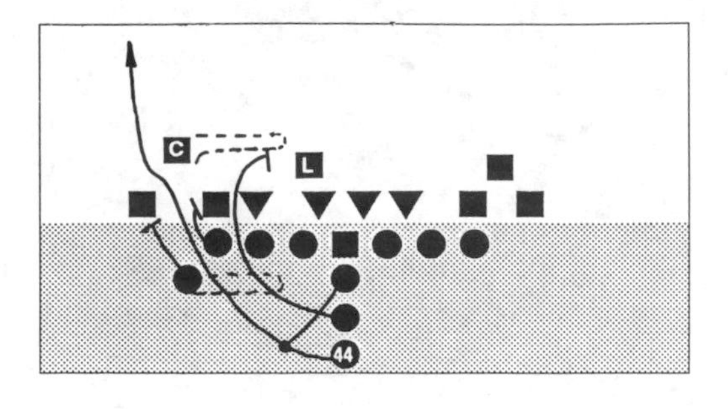

What should have been a first-down play became a backbreaker for the Dolphins. As Didier went into motion, he was followed by Miami's right cornerback, who slipped as he followed Didier's reverse motion. Riggins ran through that hole all the way for a touchdown.

MARCUS ALLEN "OFF TACKLE PLAY"

Marcus Allen, the Raiders' fine running back, ran for a 74-yard touchdown on this off-tackle play in Super Bowl XVII against the Redskins. It was one of the biggest plays in Super Bowl history, and spelled the end for the Redskins.

In this play, the tight end (lined up on

the left side) and the strongside tackle double-team the defensive end, and the tight end continues to seal off the middle linebacker; the fullback blocks the strongside linebacker; the weakside tackle pulls to help block the middle linebacker or a defensive tackle; and the weakside guard pulls, reads the fullback's block, and leads through the hole to confront the most dangerous defender. Quarterback Jim Plunkett reverses out and hands the ball to Allen, who turns to the outside, then cuts behind the fullback's block. In Super Bowl XVIII, Allen initially ran to the sideline, but before cutting upfield, he reversed backward and cut behind a block in the middle of the line.

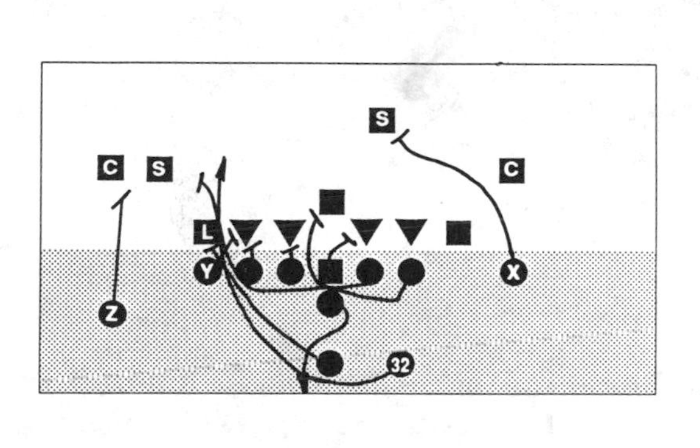

Indianapolis Colt running back Eric Dickerson runs the "28 toss" play.

ERIC DICKERSON 28 TOSS

Eric Dickerson of the Indianapolis Colts sometimes runs this play against a 3–4 defense seven or eight times a game.

The tight end blocks the strongside outside linebacker; the strongside tackle and guard double-team the defensive end and ride him inside or out. Then the strongside tackle continues on to take the strongside inside backer. The quarterback pitches to Dickerson, who runs parallel to the line of scrimmage away from the strong safety. Dickerson's movement forces the defense to string itself out toward the sidelines. The Colts' blockers continue riding them out toward the sideline. Dickerson has the option of cutting outside or inside the tight end's block and heading upfield.

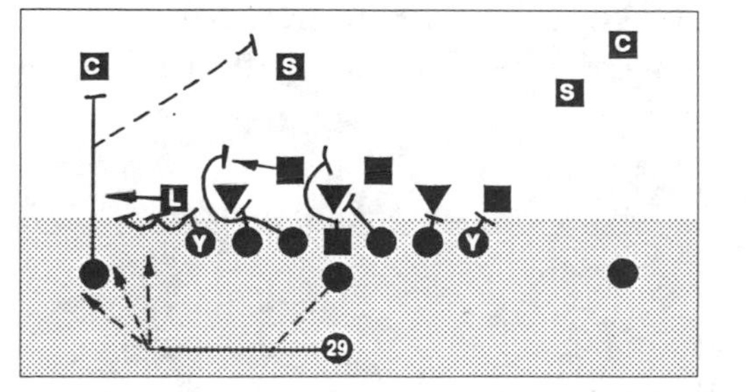

CHAPTER EIGHT

Today's Coaches' Favorite Plays

GEORGE SEIFERT, SAN FRANCISCO 49ERS

Out Pattern to Jerry Rice. Jerry Rice of the 49ers caught 49 touchdown passes in his first four seasons in the NFL, a record pace that will put him in the Hall of Fame if he keeps it up. This is one of the 49ers' most successful plays. Rice runs 20 yards and does an "out." Quarterback Joe Montana fades back and throws to Rice as he's making his cut.

San Francisco's wide receiver Jerry Rice catches a pass on an "out" pattern.

Bll Walsh, San Francisco 49ers

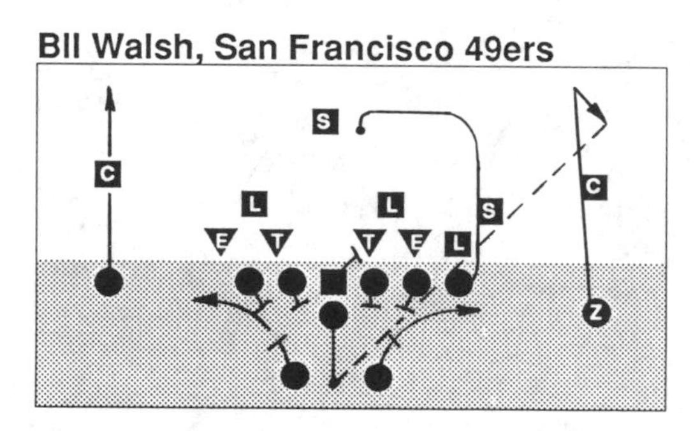

DON SHULA, MIAMI DOLPHINS

Double Wing All Go. "This 'go' pattern has been very successful for us over the past few years," says Don Shula. (A "go" pattern is one in which the receiver simply runs straight upfield.) "It's good versus zone or man-to-man coverage or the blitz. The quarterback and receivers make the necessary adjustments, and No. 13 [Dan Marino] does a great job of reading defenses and getting rid of the ball."

Don Shula, Miami Dolphins

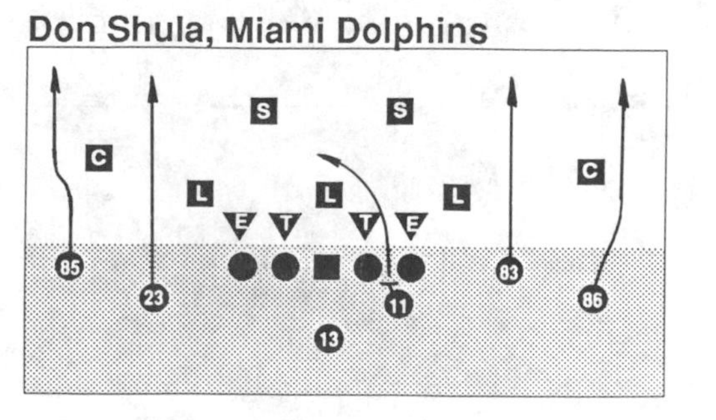

Miami Dolphin quarterback Dan Marino executes the "double wing all go" pass play.

CHUCK KNOX, SEATTLE SEAHAWKS

Weakside Off Tackle Run. Chuck Knox may be the NFL's best coach of the running game, and this is his favorite play. "If I were allowed to run one play, it would be the fullback slant to the weakside. In my opinion, it's the one great play in football. The quarterback turns and hands off to the fullback, who runs at the outside leg of the left tackle and breaks to daylight. In the 26 years I have been coaching in the NFL, our backs have made a lot of yardage on this play." Some of them are Matt Snell of the New York Jets, Mel Farr and Steve Owens of the Detroit Lions, Lawrence McCutcheon of the Los Angeles Rams, Joe Cribbs of the Buffalo Bills, and John L. Williams of the Seattle Seahawks.

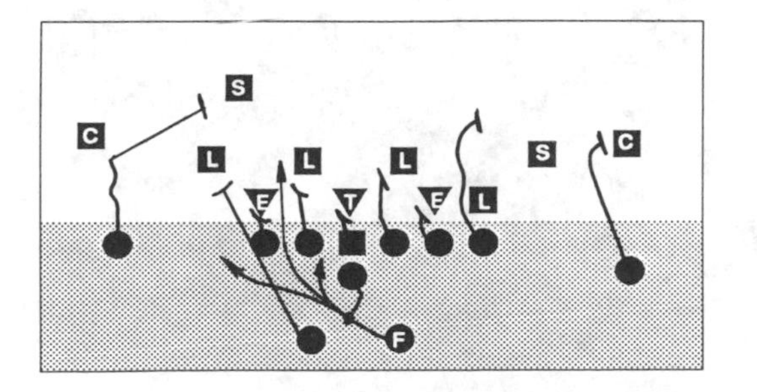

RAYMOND BERRY, NEW ENGLAND PATRIOTS

Short Passing Game. Raymond Berry was one of the NFL's greatest receivers ever, and became one of the league's best passing-game coaches. On this play, the progression in which the quarterback looks to his receivers is "X" to "A" to "Y." In other words, he will look to pass to "A" only if "X" is not open, and "Y" if "A" is also covered. "X" runs 10 yards and cuts square out; "A" runs four yards and hooks, and "Y" runs across five yards deep looking to get open over the middle.

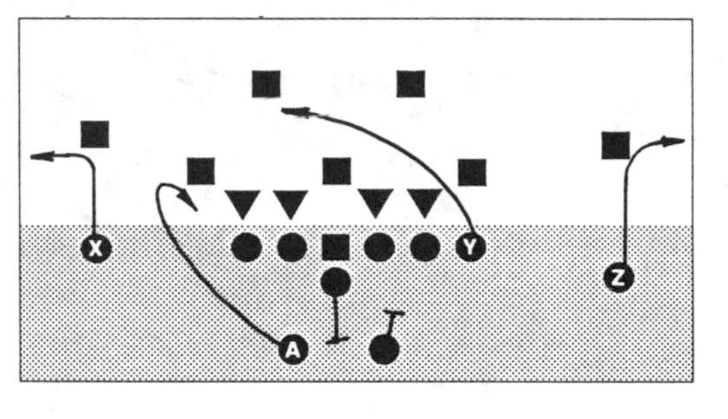

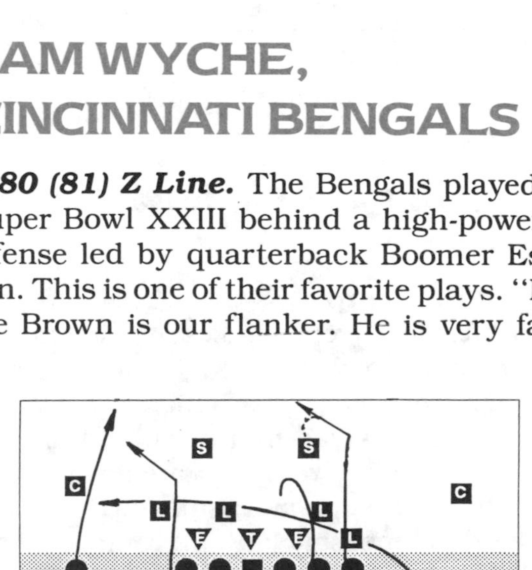

SAM WYCHE, CINCINNATI BENGALS

80 (81) Z Line. The Bengals played in Super Bowl XXIII behind a high-powered offense led by quarterback Boomer Esiason. This is one of their favorite plays. "Eddie Brown is our flanker. He is very fast,

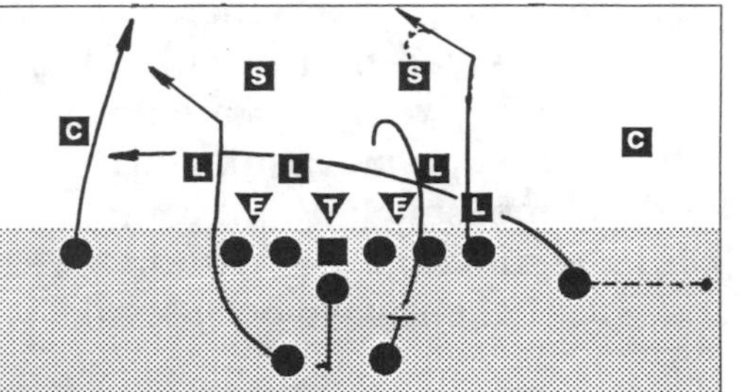

and we take every opportunity to get him the ball running across the field," says coach Sam Wyche. "The other featured receiver in this play is the halfback. We feel we have one of the best pass-receiving halfbacks in the league in James Brooks, and we try to design down-the-field patterns for him, which this play does."

BUDDY RYAN, PHILADELPHIA EAGLES

Passing Against Man Coverage and Zone Coverage. Randall Cunningham has become the most dangerous quarterback in pro football under coach Buddy Ryan, and he has three excellent receivers in Mike Quick, Cris Carter, and Keith Jackson. This diagram shows the difference in pass routes between man coverage and zone coverage. Quick ("X") and Carter ("Z") run 12 yards and cut in versus the zone and then toward the sideline against man-to-man. Against a zone, Jackson ("Y") runs five yards then slants toward the middle before doing a curl; versus man coverage, he runs the same slant, then loops back to shake his defender.

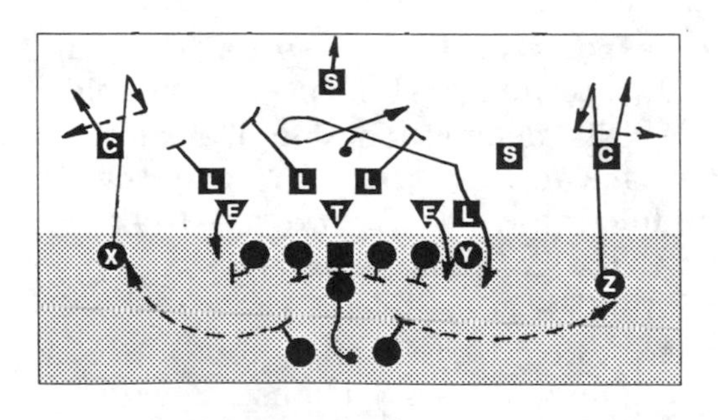

MARTY SCHOTTENHEIMER, KANSAS CITY CHIEFS

Pass Play 26. Marty Schottenheimer coached the Cleveland Browns to the playoffs from 1985 to 1988, the only NFL team to reach the playoffs in each of those years. He's now head coach of the Kansas City Chiefs, but his offense still looks the same. On this play, the tight end is lined up left and runs a post route. The two wide receivers are lined up right. The flanker goes in motion to his left, then runs an out, while the other receiver runs an up, like a bomb. The quarterback throws to whoever is open.

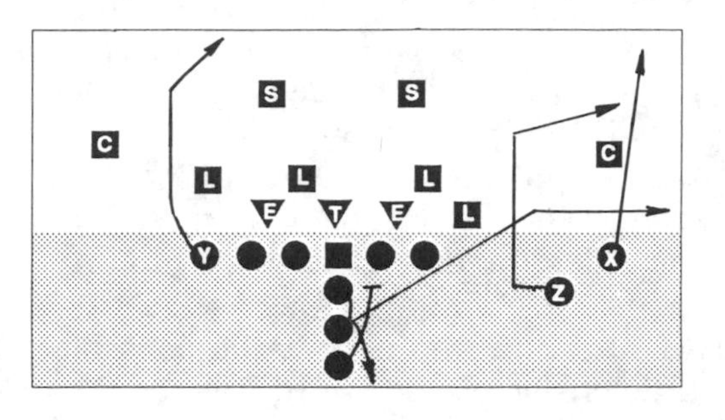

MARV LEVY, BUFFALO BILLS

Goal-Line Play. The Buffalo Bills quickly became one of the best teams in the NFL when Marv Levy took over as head coach in the middle of the 1986 season. This goal-line play was very successful for them in 1988, as Robb Riddick scored several of his 12 touchdowns using it. The Bills use two tight ends, with the flanker going in motion across the field before the snap to block the left cornerback. Quarterback Jim Kelly hands off to Riddick, who dives between the right guard and tackle.

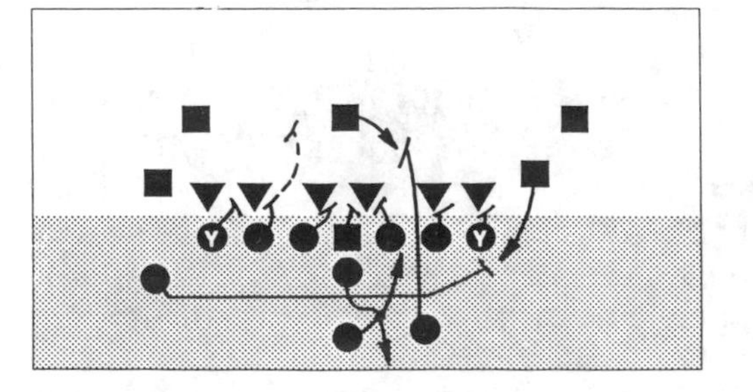

Glossary

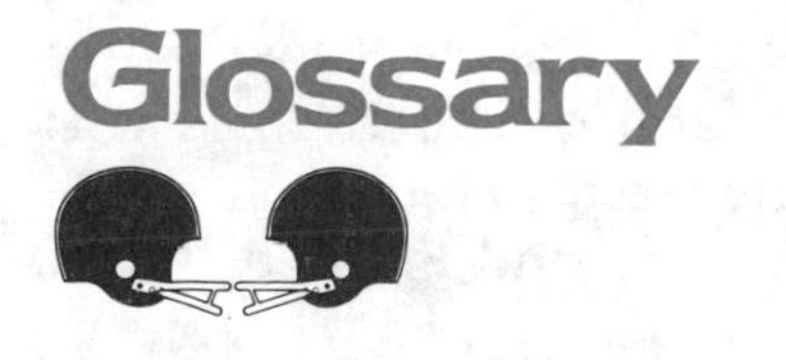

audible A play change shouted in code at the line of scrimmage. *See page 19.*

A-formation An early offense developed by Steve Owen, coach of the New York Giants. *See page 11.*

blindside The tackle of a quarterback from behind as he sets up to pass. *See page 7.*

blitz A pass rush by the defensive backs and linebackers or by the defensive backs individually. *See pages 39–40.*

bomb A long pass. *See page 43.*

bootleg The quarterback fakes a handoff, then hides the ball against his hip and runs around one of the ends. *See page 28.*

bump and run To hinder the pass receiver, the defensive player bumps him as he comes off the line, then trails him downfield. *See page 42.*

counter (misdirection) A play in which one or more backs move away from the point of attack. *See page 27.*

coverage Pass defense. Also describes the exact type of pass defense used, such as "zone defense." *See pages 42–43.*

cross block When two offensive linemen cross each other to block each other's man. *See page 17.*

dime defense A pass defense with six defensive backs. *See page 44.*

dive An offensive play designed for short gains. *See page 24.*

double coverage Two defensive players cover one receiver. *See page 44.*

double team Two offensive blockers play against one defender. *See pages 7, 17, 39.*

double wing A formation with two wide receivers on each side and only the halfback in the backfield behind the quarterback. *See page 10.*

down-and-distance The down and distance to reach a first down usually determines game strategy. *See pages 5, 15–16.*

draw A fake pass play whereby the quarterback drops back to pass, drawing the defense into pass coverage, then hands the ball to a back who runs through the gap left by the defenders. *See page 25.*

drop The movement of the quarterback as he retreats into the backfield to pass. On defense, the movement of a linebacker as he moves back into pass coverage.

Five-Three Defense An early defense which reduced the number of defensive linemen to five. *See page 35.*

Five-Two Defense (Eagle Defense) A 5-2-4 defense developed by Eagles Coach Earle "Greasy" Neale in the 1940s. *See page 36.*

flanker The wide receiver on the tight end's side of the field. A member of the backfield who must set up one yard back from the line of scrimmage. *See page 30.*

flare pass A short pass to a running back. Usually in the flat. *See page 21.*

flat The backfield area near the sidelines. *See page 29.*

flea-flicker A term originally devised to describe a passing gadget play in which a receiver, immediately after catching a pass, laterals the ball to a trailing teammate. *See page 32.*

flex defense A defense with linemen staggered on and off the line of scrimmage. Defense pioneered by Tom Landry's Dallas Cowboys. *See page 38.*

flood To put more receivers than defenders in one area of the field. *See page 30.*

fly pattern A long pass pattern where a wide receiver runs full speed downfield.

force The defensive action of a safety or cornerback to turn a running play toward the middle of the field. *See pages 41–42.*

four-three defense A defense with four linemen and three linebackers. *See pages 37–38.*

front A defensive front or front line, such as four linemen in a 4-3 defense. *See page 5.*

gadgets and gimmicks Trick offensive plays used to disrupt the defense. *See pages 32–33.*

gaps The space between two offensive linemen. A defense with a man covering gaps.

hangtime The length of time a kick stays in the air. *See pages 47–48.*

hole The space opened by blockers for a runner. Or a numbered space in the offensive line. *See pages 17–18.*

huddle A brief gathering for play called by the offense and the defense between plays. *See page 16.*

interference A penalty called when either an offensive or defensive player interferes with another player's opportunity to catch a pass.

isolation block A delayed block by a back on a defensive lineman who has been left uncovered. *See page 18.*

I-formation An offensive set-up where the backs line up directly behind the quarterback. *See pages 14, 27.*

key An alignment or movement that can tell a player where the ball is going or what blocks to expect. *See pages 18, 34–35.*

lead block A block by a running back leading another running block. *See page 18.*

man in motion An offensive formation with one man in motion. *See pages 11, 12.*

man-to-man A pass defense in which each defender is assigned to a specific receiver for the entire play. *See pages 42–43.*

nickel defense A defense with five defensive backs. *See page 44.*

nose tackle The lone tackle in a 4-3 defense who lines up "nose-to-nose" with the offensive center. *See page 7.*

Notre Dame box An offensive formation designed by Knute Rockne. *See page 11.*

onside kick A short kickoff that carries just beyond the required 10 yards to allow the kicking team a good chance to recover the free ball.

option pass A play in which the quarterback has the option of throwing to any one of a number of receivers. Or a play in which the runner has an option to run or pass, and passes. *See page 30.*

out pattern (sideline) Pass pattern where the receiver breaks toward the sideline at an angle. *See page 19.*

over defense A defense that places more men on the strong side of the offensive attack. *See page 38.*

passing tree A diagram, tree-shaped, to show pass routes. *See pages 18–19.*

pitch A long underhanded toss, usually from a quarterback to a running back. *See pages 24–25.*

play action Offensive play where the quarterback fakes a run then passes. *See page 29.*

pocket The protected area around a quarterback formed by his blockers as he passes. *See pages 16, 29–30.*

post pattern A pass route that is run straight downfield near the sideline, then breaks inside toward the goal post. *See page 19.*

power sweep The ball carrier takes a handoff from the quarterback and runs parallel to the line of scrimmage, then turns the corner behind blockers. *See pages 13, 24.*

prevent defense A defense with eight defensive backs used to "prevent" long pass completions. *See page 45.*

pro set Offensive formation that includes a quarterback, two running backs, two wide receivers, and a tight end. *See page 9.*

pull When an offensive lineman (usually a guard) leaves his position to lead a play.

read To see a key on offense or defense and interpret it. *See pages 8, 43*

red dog Pass rush by linebackers. *See page 39.*

reverse A running gadget play in which the quarterback hands off to a ball carrier going by in the opposite direction. There are a number of variations. *See pages 32–33.*

rollout The action of the quarterback as he moves across the backfield sideways to set up to pass. *See page 30.*

sack When the quarterback is tackled in the backfield by an opposing pass rusher before he can throw a pass.

safety valve Someone the quarterback can pass to in case the primary receiver is covered. *See page 5.*

screen pass A delayed passing play in which a run is faked and the ball is thrown to a running back or receiver behind the line of scrimmage. *See pages 29–30.*

scrimmage (line of) The imaginary line running from sideline to sideline through the ball before it is snapped.

seam The areas between defensive zones.

secondary The defensive backfield area and/or defensive personnel.

shift The movement of two or more offensive players before the ball is snapped. Also applies to the defensive team.

shotgun An offensive formation in which the quarterback takes the center snap at least four yards behind the center. *See page 14.*

single wing An offensive formation invented around 1906 by Pop Warner. The tailback (a deep back) takes a long snap from center in this formation. *See pages 9–10.*

slant In the slant formation, the running back runs at a slant or angle toward the hole. Also a defensive term. *See pages 19, 25.*

special teams Offensive and defensive teams that specialize in kickoffs, punts, extra points, and field goal situations. *See pages 46–49.*

spread An offensive formation with no running backs in the backfield.

stack When a linebacker stands directly behind a defensive lineman.

strongside The side of the offensive formation with the tight end or flanker, or with two wide receivers.

stunt A planned rush by linebackers and defensive linemen, or by linemen alone, in which they loop around each other instead of charging straight ahead.

sweep *See power sweep. Also pages 50–52.*

Three-Four Defense A defensive formation in which three linemen rush and a linebacker is kept in reserve as a potential blitzer on the front line. *See page 37.*

trap An offensive play in which one guard allows a defensive lineman to penetrate the backfield. Then he is blocked out by another guard from the opposite side. *See page 26.*

triple wing Similar to double wing but places three receivers to one side of the center. *See page 10.*

turmoil play An offensive play, developed by the Redskins, in which running backs, tight ends, and wide receivers all move in predetermined different directions before the snap. This often confuses the defense and frees the quarterback. *See page 32.*

turnover When the offensive team gives up the ball to the defensive team through error, such as an interception.

T-formation An offensive formation first used by the Chicago Bears. The modern T-formation put the quarterback under the center for the first time. *See pages 12–13.*

Umbrella Defense Devised by New York Giants coach Steve Owen and his defensive captain Tom Landry in 1950. *See page 36.*

under defense Opposite of over defense. The defensive line shifts away from the strongest point of attack. *See page 38.*

veer An offensive running play whose direction is determined by the reaction of the defensive linemen. *See page 25.*

weakside The side of the offensive formation without the tight end and only one receiver. *See pages 4, 8.*

wedge blocking Straight-ahead shoulder-to-shoulder blocking where more than one offensive lineman converge on a defensive player to block him out. *See page 17.*

wide receiver Usually the team's fastest receivers. They are "split"—stationed several yards from the interior linemen. *See page 6.*

zone coverage A defensive backfield alignment in which areas of the field are covered rather than a specific individual. *See pages 43–44.*

Y0-BPW-167